THIS FOOTSTOOL EARTH

THIS FOOTSTOOL EARTH

A NOVEL

JOHN ZEUGNER

RESOURCE *Publications* • Eugene, Oregon

THIS FOOTSTOOL EARTH
A Novel

Resource Publications
An Imprint of Wipf and Stock Publishers
199 W. 8th Ave., Suite 3
Eugene, OR 97401

www.wipfandstock.com

PAPERBACK ISBN: 978-1-5326-1923-6
HARDCOVER ISBN: 978-1-4982-4546-3
EBOOK ISBN: 978-1-4982-4545-6

Manufactured in the U.S.A.   09/11/18

Thus says the Lord:
"Heaven is My throne
And earth is My footstool.
Where is the house that you will build Me?
And where is the place of My rest?
For all those things My hand has made
And all those things exist," says the Lord.
"But on this one will I look
On him who is poor and of a contrite spirit,
And who trembles at My word.
He who kills a bull is as if he slays a man,
He who sacrifices a lamb, as if he breaks a dog's neck.
He who offers a grain offering, as if he offers swine's blood:
He who burns incense, as if he blesses an idol.
Just as they have chosen their own ways,
And their soul delights in their abominations.
So I will choose their delusions,
And bring their fears on them;
Because, when I called, no one answered,
When I spoke they did not hear;
But they did evil before My eyes,
And chose that in which I do not delight."

Isaiah, 66: 1-4.

Contents

I: A, B, C, Beginning

A AND B AND C are gathered now for lunch at Trattoria Serena, a small restaurant about three blocks from the front entrance of Keio University in Tokyo. A is a Brit who teaches International Law at Keio, and pursues, surreptitiously, a second career as a real estate speculator. B heads a Volkswagen dealership in the Roppongi area of Tokyo and energetically carries on with various attractive women who intersect his administrative life. Both A and B have Japanese wives. C is an older resident of what the Japanese call "Silver Housing" in a place he has named The Compound. The three ex-pat men meet regularly (every forty days or so) to talk about death. They never plan to talk about death, but somehow the conversation always ends up there. A and B are in their early sixties; C is seventy-eight. C likes to think of himself as the "rapporteur" of the group and sometimes when back at The Compound he imagines that the discussion had significance and wisdom. For several months C has been sharing with A and B a novel he is writing about death in several, not-quite fictional families. A and B are not encouraging toward C's writing. They find his texts overlong and lacking narrative tension, his tentative title: "The Riches of This World," pretentious. As a result, they rely on what he tells them of his writing, not much on the actual prose. Despite their evident reservations, C often still reads his narratives to them. Today C has promised to reveal Lewis's death.

1

The food at Trattoria Serena, like the discussion, is pallid, tepid, served in rather small portions, but always nicely presented, arranged carefully on the polished bone-white oval plates. At least twice at these luncheons B gets a phone call that requires him to go outside for privacy. A says to C: "She keeps him on a very short leash." Both chuckle with envy.

Today C initiates the discussion with an illustration: two vertical lines drawn on his small pocket notebook's third page. "Between the lines," C explains, "Woody Allen says resides human consciousness. In front of the first line and after the second line, there is only infinite nothingness. Thus, we are alive between two infinities, empty voids. Now my question is, is that correct and perhaps better, what do you think about that illustration from your vantage point: that of a competent, truly bi-cultural person?"

B says, "I don't think about it at all. It's a silly notion. I doubt Woody Allen actually said it or drew it."

After a while, A says, "I think I see what you're getting at. Maybe the Japanese concept of Akai Ito, the red thread of fate, extending presumably back into the first void and forward into the second, has some relevance. Is that what you're thinking?"

B continues, "It's not worth thinking about. It's silly."

A asks of C, "If it's truly silly why are you asking it?"

"I'm worried that human consciousness might just be an absurd flicker between two endless darknesses. How can we live knowing that, believing that? I mean, how could we? Hi there! I'm just flickering between two endless voids. Great meeting you! And now back to my endless void. I come out of void and after a brief interlude slip back into the pure void of nothingness. But I sure love it now-- lust after it, find in it the true meaning of my somewhat truncated life."

A says, "Are you complaining about living? I mean about existing."

"Was I complaining? I never meant to. Only to get at what was really important."

"You mean the after-life?" B says, "Couldn't you find solace and message in a dental office somewhere, among the magazines littering the place?"

A says, "I haven't been able to, but I could tell you about the magazines at my Meguro Cat Clinic. They're weird—pet magazines with how-to-trim-nails kinds of articles. How to brush kitty's teeth, etc. How to soften kitty's stools. Here we are, awaiting our angel hair pasta." which A pronounces the British way, as 'paster'. "So perhaps it is not of grave concern, pun intended."

C continues, "I'm so much closer to the void than you both. That's why I'm concerned."

"Take Valium or some other happy pill," B says. And then after a bit of a pause. "Once during a hockey game, I was knocked unconscious and I had the bizarre feeling that I separated from my body and was looking down, wondering why I couldn't get up, but not much caring either, and despite the shock feeling pretty good, almost wonderful, actually thinking it's sad I can't get up, but it's a whole lot better feeling good watching and wondering what might come next. Then someone shouted my name and I could get up. Is that what you are talking about? Wondering about?"

A says, "I don't think that's what he's talking about, thinking about. Is it?"

"That could be it, if I knew what it is we're seeking." C answers.

A continues, "Let me tell you about my cat Daisy's last moments. It's the most vivid experience I've had with death."

"I think I'm allergic to Daisy," B says. "But I have no objection to hearing about her last moments. In fact, thinking about her passing has already cleared my nasal passages. So, tell us about her last moments."

"Daisy's last moments—perhaps too momentous a listing. —" A muses.

"Maybe, 'The End of Allergy,' is a better listing?" B says. "Or maybe, 'The Daisy Cleanse.' In the states everybody is mad for 'cleanse' or so it seems, that and some strange plant that guarantees weight loss."

"You show little respect for a favored pet," A says. "It could be construed as heartless. I'll punish you by forbidding you from taking the next phone call."

"Not your choice," B answers.

"About Daisy's expiration?" C says.

"It began with vomiting. Not the usual cat upchucking. Hair balls and the like. But rather extensive, continuous vomiting—a signal that something more fundamental was occurring. Enough accumulation and cleanup to signal a trip to Meguro."

"You've ordered new *tatami* already?" B says.

"Of course," A replies, "but our vet, Madame Vincouvier, about seventy years old and with an amazing stacked shock of grey and very curly hair, insisted a cleanse would restore Daisy to her peak health for an animal of 'such advanced age.'"

"What we might ask," C says, "was a French woman veterinarian doing in Meguro, unless of course, she'd been there for over six decades."

"Of course, she had. Haven't we all? Aren't we all honorary Japanese with annual visas?

"Thank God for Seoul's proximity," A says. And for more than a moment conversation ceases as each relives the latest quick round trip to Seoul for a visa renewal. A recalls his miserable night at a Korean *yogwan*, adjusting his sitting on the fire-hot floor. B remembers the dazzling quickness of Wi-Fi in his five-star hotel, and C recalls his overnight with his wife's oldest friend, a language teacher living an hour out from the Seoul; her two rambunctious sons, aged five and seven, kept him up well past midnight. C reflected it was such shared discombobulations of seeking permission to live in Japan that kept the group together past all imagining—a kind of desperation of companionship and shared inconvenience. And now, C thought, it is death itself that threads us together. The vaunted red thread A mentioned ties us to Seoul's visa renewal and the certainty of expiration at some point, perhaps over the Japan Sea, could that be it?

A continues, "Ah Madame Vincouvier, surely the wisest of all the cat vets in Kanto and surely the most thorough. 'A little cleanse for your Daisy and voila! She'll be bright as new, as lithe as the lolloping leopards. And if the cleanse doesn't work, we have lots of options, and we'll explore them all till she's as right as rain, as thrilled and thrilling as any kitten in Tokyo.'"

"And how much did the cleanse cost?" B asks.

"Five hundred dollars. Daisy spent two nights in Meguro." A answers, betraying a miniscule flash of discomfort at the mention of price. "But that was just the start. The flush didn't work, didn't sweep into oblivion the shards of innards knotting. In a week I took her back to Meguro and Madame Vincouvier revealed herself to be compassion's most blossoming agent, with, evidently, a near limitless sympathy for Daisy's plight. Three more days of intravenous injections and finally a diagnosis that diabetes had complicated Daisy's intestinal aggravations. But she was responding well to the antibiotics and the loving Meguro evening massages."

"Massages?" B asks, incredulous.

"Yes. Cat shiatsu, ever heard of it? The gentlest and most expensive conceivable."

"And Madame Vincouvier spent evening after evening reading about cat digestion in her linoleum-lined room above the clinic in Meguro? Say it isn't so?" C says. Then answers himself. "Alone with her copy of Proust and her clinical studies while the Yamanote-sen rattles nearby and Daisy rests beneath her manipulating fingers."

"Not at all. Vincouvier insisted on the best masseuse in Tokyo, a spry elderly Japanese woman named Yamaguchi, who cost only one *mahn* for each eight-minute treatment. And at the end Daisy, she argued, was purring. But I didn't hear that ever. On the contrary when I brought poor Daisy home she continued vomiting and lying in the mock leather lounge chair I myself had used to recover after my rotator cuff operation. I remember leaning down toward sleeping Daisy and wanting, ever wanting, to hear the music of her purr, but nothing— only the rasp of uneven breath and an occasional very low moan. Nine *mahn* into massages and nothing like even a mild improvement."

"Nine *mahn*?" B asks, "nine *mahn* for a cat?"

'Madame Vincouvier is a very *erai sensei*, a very, very *erai sensei*."

"I don't give a damn. I'd hesitate to spend nine *mahn* on my mother, let alone my cat."

"You have a cat?" C asks

"Am I nuts?" B answers.

"You ought to understand that Daisy has been with us from the very start, right after I met Sanae," A says.

"Longevity is some kind of exoneration, justification for excessive care?"

"There is no escape from care—even you must sense that. Even you. But the point is extraneous. What is pertinent was Madame Vincouvier's passion to heal Daisy, to prolong her tired existence on this mortal plain. Her devotion to Daisy's well-being. That's what I responded to, what inevitably I bankrolled."

C says, "You thought, here is something I can care for, something worth devoting my life too? Was that it?"

"Of course, that was it. What else could anyone say?" B says.

A says, "I'm only saying that after a long time caring for Daisy I wasn't prepared to simply walk away. Who could have? And Madame Vincouvier radiated such concern that anyone would have responded to that. And there was Daisy looking so pathetic and imploring for some relief, some gesture of continuing care."

"Out of shame or guilt or both," B says.

"But," A continues, "even Madame Vincouvier failed to convince her staff, and that failure shifted opinion about Daisy's future . . . It began with her suggestion that further tests were important, despite the expense already invested in the various rescue procedures—all of which had fallen short. So now she argued that Daisy needed an ambulance trip to Sendai for an MRI, yes, a cat MRI. Cost? Approximately *ni jeu mahn yen*. Yes, two thousand dollars U.S. to find out that Daisy was dying, had been dying, as do we all, from the moment she was born." A looks around sheepishly, imagining he has enunciated the most obvious yet most hidden remark. "But to grant Madame Vincouvier some self-consciousness, she said to me, and loud enough for her staff to hear, 'But I suppose, that is an expense more than you may be willing to undertake, given all that her illness has already inflicted on you.'"

"Perhaps you had informed her Daisy's costs had already prevented your boat payment?" B asks smiling, then laughing.

"Not precisely," A answers, "but spiritually quite correct. I muttered something about Daisy being at least twenty years old—for a cat in Japan, well beyond lifetime expectation. Far longer than my own. And Madame Vincouvier nodded, but seemed disappointed and with somewhat sharpness said, 'Well, take her home and let God resolve the situation. I apologize for inflicting such unwelcome expenses on you already. I often misjudge an owner's commitment to his pet. I suppose you have spent something like fifteen hundred dollars U.S. by now. It would be untoward to ask for more. Staff will help you get Daisy back into her travel cage.' And there was exemplary gentleness in staff's lifting of Daisy back into her towel-lined wire and wood travel cage. She cowered at the end of the box, on her green fluffy Turkish towel.

"And for a couple of days Daisy seemed better. She neither vomited nor moaned at all. But I noticed she bloated again and by the third day I began to worry that she was not normally excreting or urinating at all. I enticed her with green tea, even warm milk, but she stopped eating or drinking, as if trying herself to tame the bloating. She slept on her side and her visible limbs just extended straight out from her swollen body, as if directing an invisible tide, a wind from somewhere she alone could experience. And then a quiet, very quiet occasional whimper. So, it has come at last, I thought. And I face-timed with Nigel who, as the youngest, had been closest to Daisy. He was in pajamas (something he'd never worn as a child) and said sweetly, 'She looks bad. Looks like the end. That must be tough for you, Dad. How does Madame feel about euthanasia?' I was surprised he remembered Vincouvier. 'She's a fierce interventionist,' I answered, 'not inclined to give up for any reason.' 'How French,' Nigel said, 'argumentative to the end. So, here's my advice—don't deal with her at all. Seek out one of the Japanese assistants and say the following, I mean this, precisely. Say it just as I'm telling you now. Put Daisy in the assistant's arms and say quietly but with absolute conviction and authority, 'In my dream last night Daisy said to me that it was time and I should ease her into the next phase. She said that to me, and now you must help me. I put Daisy entirely in your hands and I need your help easing her out of this painful life. I'm so sorry, so very sorry, but you must prepare Daisy for exit from this life, and bring her back to me so I can hold her as she eases out of her misery.' Emphasize how much you will be indebted to the assistant for this favor, and, if necessary, say that Madame has authorized it. That may not be necessary. I suspect the assistant will believe that, and act on it with visible relief.' As I listened to him, his phrase, *visible relief,* flooded into me. 'And how do you know all this, Nigel?' 'Mom told me before she left—she said, 'your father won't be able to snuff Daisy. You'll have to show him, instruct him, each step of the way. He'll need that, and you can do it. It's natural for you and me, but not for him.''

"Self-serving," B says.

"Oh, doubtless so," A answers, "but in fact Nigel was absolutely correct. I knew Madame Vincouvier was a late riser and came to her cat clinic in the later morning, but the assistants were there from 7:30. So I brought my swollen, bloated, moaning Daisy in by eight o'clock, and I spoke with Ms. Tomoko just as Nigel had instructed me. I said *'gomen'* a number of times, and flashed my most humbling ' *onegai shimasu'* again and again. We all understand, don't we that in Japan apology precedes everything else. But here was an interesting case where apology apparently collided with authoritarian hierarchy. They were scared to act without Madame's steady imprimatur. But Nigel knew, and I came to understand, the fundamental compassion of underlings would eventually triumph over remembered directives. The situation at hand would cloud over the rulings from all authority. Japan lives that every moment. Here I was with the pathetic and wonderfully moaning kitty. Who would not be turned toward helping? They carried poor Daisy directly to the young junior vet inspecting a tightly collared Dachshund at the far end of the reception room. . He felt Daisy's bloated stomach, pinched a few places, and listened as the technicians rattled off the saga of previous treatments. And quickly the fellow got up from his haunch position, carried Daisy to a back room and in a trice reappeared with her right forepaw swathed in purple adhesive tape, holding an inserted IV tube. The technician behind him carried a large, ominous looking syringe, full, I presumed, of death. 'Follow me' the young vet said in a strangely un-Asian accent and I thought perhaps he's a dark New Zealander or perhaps someone from Guam or Samoa. I followed him, and we went into a room with three club-like booths upholstered in a green Naugahyde. He slid into the first booth and put Daisy at the center of the table. I slid into the other side. Two attendants stood like waiters at the end of the table. 'I will inject. You may pet her and watch her. Look at her eyes, if you like. It will be over very quickly.' There was no time for me to say much of anything, arrange much of anything. I was thinking perhaps a towel under her would have been more comfortable, but in truth she seemed groggy and foggy, although she did turn her head toward me, plopped on her very inflated side. She licked momentarily toward her nose, blinked. He bent her leg to an angle more receptive for his syringe. He was moaning softly— apparently what he imagined were comforting tones. Were these Buddhist tones to accompany voyage to some next phase, next arena for re-appearance? Daisy as something else. I tried to think what else, but I imagined nothing for her. Could it be animals had no animus for transformation? It seemed I had read that some place. His moaning got louder, and I did stare into Daisy's eyes, which already no longer seemed clear or focused. But it did seem she acknowledged me. He eased whatever was in the syringe into her IV tube, and within a second Daisy made the first sound I had heard her make on this last day. She gave out a miniscule sigh, a little tiny unimaginable rasp that momentarily filled the booth, the room, the very air we were breathing, and then, stone glare of eyes gone eerily clear and coldly marble. I continued to pet her side until he said, firmly, resolutely. 'She's gone.'" I thought but didn't say, I've been with her for over 20 years.

B says, "And disposal?"

Before that inquiry could be answered the side door to Trattoria Serena opens and, most remarkably, a tall woman with a great shock of curly grey hair enters the tiny restaurant. "Madame Vincouvier," A says in evident amazement. His voice is hushed and strangely reverent, even for a moment guilty, or so C imagines.

Madame Vincouvier recognizes A and comes over to his table. "You disappoint me often but never more so with your disgusting going behind my back to do what? To kill an innocent healthy creature who depended on you for life and sustenance over, what? Over twenty years, or so you told me— as if I cared. I never dreamed you were such a monster, such a grotesque version of humanity, such a dreg! And I see normal human commerce has not changed an iota for you. Here you are among so called friends, enjoying a rich repast while the ashes of your charge doubtless are littering up some children's park in Ueno. It boggles the mind.

How little we pay to the basic building block of all good life—the extension of existence. The very force that unites us you trample on so casually, so brutally, so sickeningly. I've heard very wonderful things about this place—so aptly named. But I could never eat here, not now certainly with you here and imbibing its fellow-feeling without a tidbit of affection for your 'beloved' Daisy."

B interrupts, "I think that's quite enough. Quite enough. We all live a sham life here and it's silly the little huffs we generate to validate our continuing existence in this unfortunate milky milieu—I mean public kindness toward us. I know where your resentment comes from, and I share it. Share it. But I'm ashamed to say so. So, break off the crummy tirade. He's suffered quite enough."

Madame Vincouvier seems non-plussed by B's outburst and cocks her head to get a better view of him, then straightens her orange scarf. After such adjustment she says quietly, "Better you than Daisy," and leaves Trattoria Serena.

"Okay, then," B continues, "Tell us now about Lewis's death."

2.

Madam de Vincouvier's front room was perfumed heavily, the scent of lilac in an excess that did not quite shut out the fumes of cat urine, dog dandruff, or the salivation of creatures housed more elegantly elsewhere in Tokyo. How improbable, C often reflected as he sheepishly came through the *genkan* that a French woman in black bombazine would be the most cherished veterinarian in Kanto. How extraordinarily Japanese that she would have, beyond her ministrations to animals, a human service at once hyper closeted and liberating, relieving, gushing pain and ultimate deliverance. How he panted for her savage, severe touch.

"Is the room ready?" C asked between rushed, short breaths.

"In a moment. We must be patient. There should be an excess of light, a painful brightness, should there not?"

"Of course. Hot white light," C responded. "It's the beginning of banishing decrepitude."

"Such flowery English. Perhaps not appropriate. Perhaps irritating."

"I apologize."

"Not yet accepted," she gently laughed. "Let's have some tea and again remember Daisy. I wasn't here when A, how do you say it, 'put her down.' That wasn't thoughtful of him, was it? No, it wasn't. 'Put her down,' maybe I should do that to you? Would you like it? Why couldn't you have waited till I came in at normal office hours? Why did you hide it from me?"

"I didn't! He wanted to spare you. We knew you had affection for her, because of your long treatment of her."

"Liar! You know of course I had to fire the technician— a really gifted practitioner. How could I have tolerated such insubordination?"

"He said you would have approved. We didn't want him to lose his job."

"You didn't seem to think about the consequences of your selfishness, and yet you've lived how very long in this country where every action is measured in consequence and in soft language. It's an insipid defense. Remind me to punish you for it." She pushed the plunger of her tea plastic canister and filled two small bowls. They sat in two blue print wing chairs flanking the dark walnut door that led, he knew, to the stairs up to the all-white room.

"You really want to go up, don't you?" she pointed to the door.

"Of course! You know that better than I do."

"I know so much more than you know, especially about yourself—your tiresome needs."

"I don't wish to be tiresome."

"Nor would I let you, *mon petite choux.*"

"I know that. I do know that."

"So, we understand each other and can talk sincerely about going up. Don't tell me again, how anxious you are, how full of expectations, anticipations, deliverances that always recede as we approach them. That discussion is tiresome, more than tiresome, boring. Useless and boring." She took a long sip of the tea and then closed her eyes and rocked slowly back against the blue print of the wing chair. "I'm thinking today we need to take extreme measures, ones outside, well outside, our usual parameters. Explorations at the edge, beyond the simply extreme, rather at the cusp of the transcendent, on pain's periphery, so that insight cannot be separated from anguish. Does it interest you? Spiraling anguish. Can you feel it? Endure it? What would it reveal? More likely, what would it set free in you, in us? I'd like us to ask the key question: what could reside beyond our abominations? What would passing through them suddenly illuminate? Could we pass beyond the *tatemae* of our investigation to the actual *honne*? I think we could, and what would we find? Daisy waiting for us? Could we sacrifice a bull as if we were killing a man? Kill a lamb as if breaking a dog's neck? Burn incense as if worshiping an idol? Could we do it all?"

"Yes! Of course we could."

"And at the end of it what would our abominations reveal?"

"Quick and joyous passage through the moat. Lolloping deliverance through thick thighs of hurt."

"Offensive language again. Extra strikes against you, severe ones."

"And deserved."

"Don't be frivolous, don't be trivializing. You will suffer greatly for it."

"I'm sorry."

"Don't be sorry either. It's insulting and at the same time boring. So readily offered from your entirely manufactured and bogus sentiments. I'm here to show how disassociated your pain is, how trivial that is, compared to the searing I'm willing to inflict. Have you not seen how much you are a human being-*manqué*?"

"Not *manqué*! I'm not a bogus person."

"Such a phony objection. Unworthy of you, and garnering greater suffering no doubt. Yes, you have only a shell reality, a puppet of normality, performing normal sentiments on the mica edge of self-perceived mockery. A sham of feeling wandering after affirmation, anxious for a spanking or full-on flagellation. And yet through agonized tears recognizing its very phoniness, lack of substance, lack of conviction about anything, even the pain it wallows in. Begging to be set on fire, consumed with actual conviction, but ever never finding any." She paused, looked strangely pensive. "Maybe I really can't get you over the moat, can I?"

"You can. You have. You often have."

"But not every time, is it not so? Don't lie to me."

"Yes, not every time, but often enough."

"Often enough. . ." she mused a moment, as if counting the times. "Could we sacrifice a bull as if slaying a person?"

"Of course!"

"Kill a lamb as if breaking a dog's neck?"

"Yes!"

"Burn incense as if worshipping an idol?"

"In our white-hot room, why not?"

"Good. Let us go upstairs. And while I work, tell me, tell me slowly, how Lewis died.

II: A, B, C, Lewis Walling

THE BULLET FROM NOWHERE entered through his spleen and exited shoving segments of his stomach, intestine, pancreas and duodenum out into the rice field's still, grey water. He thought, I've been gut shot, the worst of all prospects. Shot by an unseen unrecognized enemy as alone in this special place as I am. Perhaps I wasn't the target at all. Maybe a rifle went off somewhere, having been tossed by someone ignorant of the effect, until the firing happened.

The force of the wound tossed his innards away from him, bobbing in the rice water like a cat avoiding embarrassment. His blood streamed out as if to lasso his fractured insides floating away. For a moment he imagined he could collect them still, but that attempted movement sent pain swelling through his shock and he collapsed into the water, finding only at the last minute the strength and coordination to turn his head up and aside for air. Water and gasping mixed in his bobbing search to survive.

She only opened the door about three inches. The chain lock was not visible, but he sensed she had wedged her foot against the door's edge, keeping just three inches for them to exchange slow looks. Lewis thought, I must not let my guts get away. I must gather them up and keep them close, so that repair and revival can occur. If they get away I'm lost. "You're all growed up," she said with a sweetness that reminded him of so very much. "I suppose so," he answered with what he knew she'd find *suaveness, worldly mastery, true maturity.* But he knew she didn't really care about that, only about him. He'd come to see her because he knew she cared only about him. "And how did you find me?" she said. "By looking and looking, and asking and asking," he answered, leaning closer into their three inches, trying to see her better, smell her closer. Yes, she was not open to the world. He knew that, sensed that when she left so quickly. Why did he want so much to see her now? Because she cared about him, was that truly it? Yes, truly that was it. He knew it was now the purest moment for certainty. No time, absolutely no time for obfuscation. No time for calculated response, no time for strategy. I can't reach out now to grab my guts. They're floating away, almost over the horizon.

"I'm glad you're growed up."

"So am I." He thought, why did I seek her out now? Why now? Because he knew at some level that he would die soon, could that be it? As his guts swam away he knew beforehand their outer drift well beyond seeping blood lasso; and therefore what was most precious in the future must be recovered, reaffirmed, re-celebrated, re-lived, re-stamped with indelible accent, indelible belief. So of course, he sought her out. He wanted her to know beforehand how she had shaped him, and, besides, when he thought about departure who else really mattered to him?

-§-

B interrupted him: "Who the hell are you talking about?"

A answered for C: "Annie May. Doesn't that click something for you?"

"Of course not. Why should it. A name I've never heard before."

"So, you didn't read the play. You're way behind. Naughty lad who didn't do his homework."

"What a lot of horseshit. Who has time to read a play?"

-§-

Was there someone else with her that she wouldn't let him in? He might have asked but realized it was not someone else that kept them fixed on their three inches of seeing one another. He realized her memories hardly converged with his, and that terrible separation of fulfillment kayoed any communication. She was at least 45 years old; he was 20. He was white, she was black. She had held him since he was one and one-half years old. "I wanted to see how you were. How you were getting along. And I wanted to say goodbye."

"That's good," she answered.

"You never said goodbye, but I wanted to say goodbye."

"It's been some time. Your folks didn't want me to say goodbye. Just get out I guess."

"I never understood." He said slowly not looking at her. Shame flooded in. "I'm sorry for whatever."

He couldn't breathe. He couldn't turn his head aside and up again. Sudden chill. Retching ache spiraled after his drifting insides slowly losing their pink tinge in the brown, still water. There she was rocking him in mewling pain, holding him softly in that cramped vertical striped room, rocking, creaking in the polished maple chair. He thought but was too wracked or embarrassed to say (he couldn't tell which)—you were the one I wanted to see, wanted to say goodbye to, because I doubt I'll come back, doubt I'll need to come back, or want to come back. You meant so much to me, put safety in my hands—your hands. I wanted to know you were still in this world, available in this world and here I am three inches away spreading my leaking blood lasso around whatever it was that meant so much to me. I cannot tell you, cannot say. So, I found you, after nights of looking, listening, waiting. Here I am nudging my stupidity through your door and relieved you're not letting me in. Beyond her was a gleaming light blueness, shimmering in his mind. I can speak through all embarrassment now. Yes, I can speak straight out in a way I couldn't, or wouldn't ever before. But now, but now. Now it's truly irrelevant any restriction on my saying anything. The freedom of last moments—maybe you don't feel it. But in soft grey water and drifting pain one can speak only honestly, think honestly. So here I am. Didn't biblical figures say as much? Addressed in extremis, all that could be acknowledged was Here I am, Lord. Here I am.

"It's so nice Louie for you to come by. So very nice, but I'm not in a good place just now. Not now. I sees what's troubling you, and I have saw it often, but not now."

"Saw it often," he repeated, smiling. "Saw it off, and I get it. I just wanted to see you and say goodbye. I won't come again. You don't have to worry about that. I absolve you from that worry."

"Don't say that, Louie. Don't be mean, Louie. Don't."

"What's mean about the truth?

"Don't be mean, Louie."

It's truth. I have been mean. I see that, feel that now. How cold it feels how watery cold. So let me gather back all my meanness, take it up and gather it in again, pull it toward me, ensnared in my bleeding come back to me. Healing at last as the pain drains off, spiraling elsewhere in the quiet grey pool all around. All around.

-§-

But B interrupts, "I think you're drifting off target—setting up your own hang-ups and not Lewis's. And why does she call him Louie?"

"That's what she always called him." C answers.

"Artistic license," B says brusquely. "We don't know anything about Lewis. Why should we care about his expiration in the rice paddy—itself pretty much a trite turn of events."

A says, "From the play you should have a good idea of the failure of Lewis's life. Ah, but then you haven't read the play, and not having read it, you must remain ignorant of all his motivations."

"So, tell me about the play. Maybe I can be spared the delight of plowing through it."

"It's not much delight," A says. "But it does explain a good bit. But I wonder if you really want explanation. The story is involving, or it isn't. I don't see how context or background helps anything."

"Well, I raised a question and it seems no one can answer."

"I can answer," C says, "the play details the family dysfunction that leads Lewis to join the Army—in particular it lays bare, so to speak, the peculiar way the family has of creating and buttressing and utterly inhabiting a completely bogus reality, a projection of family as might be imagined by a third rate sit-com writer who had nonetheless memorized Hallowell's Guide to Upper Class Imitation, and who passionately longed to have children able to carry milk glass rectangles of menthol cigarettes for invited guests."

"Pretty bitter ... and dated. Nobody passes cigarettes now. Nobody," B says, smiling. "So, the negress behind the chained door—"

"Not chained," C insisted, "merely foot wedged at about three inches open."

"My mistake," B continued, "and doubtless a crucial element. So, the Negress—"

"Annie May," C said.

"All right, Annie May, refuses to let Lewis in, and to explain that we need to have the play in hand. So why not put the play in before the Lewis's death account?"

"I'll take that under advisement. I had asked you to read the play beforehand."

"Requesting is not structure," B answered.

"I wanted the sweetest moment of his life to continue," C said. "The absolute sweetest, as if we could only summon that sweetness at the crucial end."

"He is a pathetic child," A interjected. "But we're pulling for him, while lamenting the lack he suffered in extremis. Can I say that?"

"You can say it, but it's a distancing I was really trying to eliminate."

"What saves us you cannot eliminate."

"Understood, but not accepted," C said. "Understood. I'll re-work his death."

-§-

Later in Meguro, at the Cat Hospital, C said to Madame Vincou-vier, "They rejected Lewis's death utterly. Were unmoved by it. And now I'll have to rework it entirely. So much energy for such disappointment."

"You poor boy," she answered. "You failed, didn't you? And not for trying hard. Indeed, you tried very, very hard, but your energy was unfocused, almost useless. Useless. You need discipline, don't you, my disappointed boy. Shall I discipline you?"

"Yes, please."

"With no easing off?"

"Yes, please, no easing off this time."

"No safety phrase stopping everything?"

"No safety phrase. Just the punishment I deserve."

"But only if you pass on your stories of Lewis's background, as well as your half-plays."

"They have them already, but already isn't all read."

"For a lame pun, punishment is all red." And Mne Vincouvier ran her tongue slowly across her upper lip.

-§-

The Riches of This World, Part A

Lewis's Back Stories in 2.2. Chapters

(Chapter One: The Toughest Bar in Worcester)

In the last, most profitable act of his Brahmin life Walter Jelliffe convinced his son, Waldo, to marry Suzan Corcoran, the slightly unhinged daughter of Worcester's richest family. That union brought Waldo the one enterprise he could fathom and embrace: publisher of Worcester's "alternative" weekly newspaper, *The New Worcester Spy*. Thus did Mayflower power fuse with the apparently limitless acquisitions flowing from Corcoran Abrasives. The linkage generated a certain amount of friction, and the titular Walter had been characteristically blunt with his son: "Anyone who marries for money earns every penny of it, but let's face it, there's *sweat-earnings* versus *suck-up earnings*. And from what I've seen of you, Waldo, the latter seems more natural, more in line with your tastes." There was a wondrous gentleness in the squeeze the old man applied to his son's shoulder and mind.

"I'll work at it, Daddy," Waldo replied. And he did. In the early years of the marriage Waldo spent hours on the fifth floor of Worcester Memorial Hospital's psych ward, listening to Suzan explain how she had made him rope sandals, and beaded leather wallets. He kept her on her lithium and constantly reassured her that given her situation she could have married almost anyone in Worcester–that he was in fact only the best of a long line of suitors. He worked hard to get her admitted to his luncheon club, The Worcester Club. It was largely through his efforts that women were eventually permitted even in the smoking rooms.

Waldo also worked hard at his publisher position–though he easily understood–as did all Jelliffes, that real work must be accomplished by others; his position and ownership was –and the phrase was his proudest editorial achievement–"residually iconic". He symbolized the sanctification of achievement by the "old line" in town. It was Walter Jelliffe himself who reiterated, after sufficient sherry, what he called John Keats' finest declaration: "A gentleman is one who is not wholly preoccupied with getting on." So Waldo, following Walter's lead, left actual actions, decisions, rewrites–in short, "getting-on" to others. He enjoyed being the final voice, never invoked, the absolute ruler whose only task was to meet the public and every now and then come up with a "brilliant feature proposal." The job left him gobs of time for slow luncheons at the club, side trips to Bermuda, early dinners with Suzan, month-long stays with her at various installations of sound mind and body. Waldo immensely enjoyed the latitude he had with *The Spy's* staff. He was at once the daffy uncle on the premises and the Zeus of certain death if you didn't play along. He was at *The Spy*, as in life itself, to be indulged. Indulgence came certainly with the Jelliffe name enforced with Corcoran monetary muscle.

Now in his fiftieth year Waldo Jelliffe had not given up the khakis of his swell collegiate life, nor the thin sweaters or cashmere blazers. He wore, as if in anticipation of his retirement years, and in recollection of his golden youth, New Balance running shoes or Timberland high tops in reverence for his New England roots even if, he noted at the club bar one night, the labor was not exactly Brahmin on Batam Island (where the shoes were made) perhaps a little swarthy even, and certainly dirt cheap. He was proud of his trip to Batam Island off the Malaysian coast, prouder still of his one single byline feature: "The Worcester/Batam Connection" in which he lovingly recorded the barracks lives of those exploited Southeast Asian laborers who sent everything they earned back home to China, India, the Philippines or wherever. Waldo had liked the spicy food and hammering Malaysian sun; he admired the way things ran so promptly and cleanly in Singapore. Worcester could learn a lot from ASEAN his one article maintained. And Kuala Lumpur was the one city on the planet he could emigrate to, he told the younger staffers and interns at *The Spy*, if circumstances should ever require him to leave Worcester. It interested him sometimes to wonder what those circumstances might be. Could he be a secret serial killer, filleting young women with one of Chef Tony's lifetime knives? He saw the knives advertised often enough on T.V., and once he had called the 800 number to inquire which of the knives would be best for gutting girls. "Be serious," the operator replied. "You want one set or two?" Most of all he liked the strange liberation he felt on Batam. It was almost as if he had lost weight or was wearing weirdly bouncing sneakers launching him farther up into the soft, mucid air. Every step seemed to radiate "Yes!" in his confident striding. There was always a troubling collapse in the return flight, as if the seat, the cramped air, the sour food was pressing down on his buoyancy, returning him to a heritage of empty strangulation. "I swear to God I'm taking you back with me, LP, (his nickname for the Vietnamese in charge of the workers barracks) just to feel alive again."

Lately he spent more and more time with the younger staffers and interns since they only imperfectly understood his irrelevance. He was for them, the owner, the publisher, the ultimate authority, who merely husbanded his power by never displaying it. They did not understand what lineage could and could not do. And they responded enthusiastically to his rare proposals. And a few of them grasped that it was through Waldo that their own ideas could percolate in *The Spy's* system.

Thus it was not exactly clear who thought the feature up but Waldo certainly embraced the great pub crawl search for "The Toughest Bar in Worcester." And he began the deliberations with what he knew was the central point: "Look, you have to have a standard, a comparison point on toughness. You've got to have a clear idea of what you mean by 'toughest'. What is the essence of 'toughness' and where do you find it? If you can point to one bar as 'tough', then you can say X or Y exceeds that standard by such and such a factor and therefore it is not yet, 'The toughest Bar in

Worcester.' And surprise of surprises, I can give us the standard: the old Valhalla Bar on Summer Street."

"It's gone–they built the new police station on the site," someone answered.

"I know that, but its perishing makes it the perfect standard. No one can really say what it was on the scale of toughness. We can establish one ourselves. Besides, when I taught at the old jail, inmates told me it was the toughest bar in town. You could always be guaranteed a fight if you went in. That's toughness. Maybe we should put a time factor into the equation. Whadya think?"

"Art's Diner on West Boylston street. The Huns hang out there."

"The Brass Helmut on Main Street---Hispanic gangs."

"Any place on Green street. Vietnamese gangs all over the place there."

Waldo objected, "We need more work on the standard. On criteria. Give me criteria.

Something to sink our teeth into. Something the lunchpails will understand."

Waldo tended to regard those who worked for a living as "lunchpails," although the term disappointed and discouraged Walter Jelliffe.

"I still think we need a time constraint," Waldo said. "You have to engage in actual fisticuffs within, say, nine minutes of entry. How does that sound?"

"You'll need a time keeper," Lewis Walling said, the most senior of the interns. There was a trace of whining sarcasm in his tone.

Waldo looked carefully at him, then finally said, "And a nifty stop watch, I suppose."

"And a hostility quotient," Walling continued, "maybe made up of equal parts rage, envy, insecurity, belief God is on your side."

"Lunch pail," Waldo answered.

"And we'd need bodyguards, people to do the actual fighting–either that or a year of combat training before we start the crawl."

Waldo and Suzan had no children, and Waldo had the habit of adopting one of the interns as the son he was convinced he didn't want. Lewis Walling was the latest in his adoptions–three previous adoptions had migrated to graduate school or Rhode Island papers. One became an editor in New Haven.

"Look, Walling, you like to throw log jams on the fire. I know that, but we can easily find a few thugs to back us up in testing the hostility. You probably know some yourself--football players or Rugby freaks."

"I do."

"Good, then let's not lock down over trivia. We need criteria-perfect criteria. A fight in nine minutes is a good start, but just a start."

"The first thirty seconds is crucial. True toughness signals itself right out of the gate. If you can't find a hostile phrase, look, gesture in 30 seconds, the place fails. We need a play book of gestures and phrases–that can be part of the article." Walling said, warming to the task.

"What about ethnicity?" Waldo asked.

"Meaning what?" Walling answered.

"Meaning should we stipulate a certain homogeneity as key to hostility. It's a Latino bar and we walk in and there's looks and so on. Does that qualify? Does the toughness have to go beyond resentment of outsiders? Isn't that natural? And therefore discountable?"

"So it has to be a WASP bar?"

"Don't be stupid." Waldo said. "We're looking for an add-on factor – something that can begin in ethnic resentment but quickly boils over into generalized hatred, a pure viciousness aimed out of the soul of bile."

"The soul of bile," Walling repeated. "The soul of bile. Something that comes out of generations of repression? The end product of remembering that this town once was the center of New England, a palace of wire manufacturing –the barbed wire kingdom of the world and then, and then, the ugly descent as Swedes gave way to Italians and Irish and then to southeast Asians–wire to plastic, to gutted factories, abandoned mills, thence to boutiques and finally to plywood–so that everybody carries around a longing for some imagined time of prosperity. What begins as resentment for skin color ends as boiling rage and blame for loss of autonomy–all over some local IPA or Miller lites? Is that it?"

"You catch on quick," Waldo laughed. "And always measured against the imagined slugfests at the old Valhalla."

"We seek the new Valhalla," Walling answered.

"Exactly!" Waldo said, "That's our title–'Seeking the new Valhalla'. Get us gladiators."

"I can get Singleton, Navy ROTC cadet commandant at Holy Cross–lots of rage just below the bellowing surface, and five or six Rugby players Singleton knows."

"Not five or six. One. One from the scrum. One large one from the scrum. Singleton plus one. Just adequate to get us out alive." Waldo smiled.

2.

The Spy's offices were on the sixth floor of a restored building on Front Street overlooking Worcester Commons. The freshly sand blasted facade of the building was directly across from the parched earth commons, grassless and flecked with grey scraps of winter snow. There was a large reflecting pool, utterly empty save for residue clumps of ice/snow and several half- crushed soda cans. Beyond the empty pool was a small graveyard with slightly twisted or turned headstones from the 18th century. And beyond the graveyard was a mammoth horse and soldier statue for the Spanish American war, prancing upward, kicking its hooves toward the plywooded and abandoned downtown aptly named Commons Fashion Outlet Mall.

When Walling and Singleton entered the Spy Building, along with Ralph (the one from the scrum) they all hurried past the little lobby area with its matching leather loveseats. Singleton had honed in on the marble sheathing over the three elevators beyond the lobby and seemed intent on reaching the seventh floor before anyone else. Walling admired Singleton's focus in this and all matters–no time to lose, no enemy too strong to be confronted, the perfect protector on any search for the toughest bar anywhere.

But Waldo from his leather loveseat headed Singleton and the rest off: "We're here ready for the charge, way ahead of you," he said, standing up and motioning to the woman still on the loveseat. "Suzan, meet our bodyguards."

Singleton, a gangly fellow probably 6 '2" or 6' 3", with a military brush cut and very thick black rimmed glasses was nonplussed by Suzan's appearance. How could you find boxing action with a woman in the entourage? The new Valhalla, a term Singleton cherished when Walling told it to him, might not have even a spot for visiting women. And on a mission women would only prove more vulnerable and difficult–didn't all his commanders acknowledge as much, although publicly they might speak quite contrarily about the admission of women into combat.

Suzan Jelliffe stood up, a delicately coiffured woman of 50, still quite thin with a longish face, too large a nose, and disturbingly vacant look to her face as if she were constantly imagining something beyond the apparent focus point of her eyes. A doorway perhaps through which would come something more interesting than things at hand. Waldo took her hand and said, "She's brought the camera."

"The camera?" Walling asked.

"Of course," Suzan said, suddenly present, "to record these events that alter and illuminate our time, together. Our little voyage into places where no one else has ever gone."

"The frolic spaces for the lunch pails," said Waldo, taking Suzan's hand.

"I thought we were hitting bars," Ralph the rugby player said.

"You'll do," Waldo said to him. "You'll do nicely. Solid, and can take a punch. He can take a punch. See Suzy, he can take a punch." And Waldo slapped him on the arm.

Walling said, "So we don't have to go upstairs?"

"Nope," Waldo said, "She's got the camera right here." He took a dark thick glasses case out of Suzan's fabric bag. "I had a hole cut for the lens–takes digital pictures–we'll get everything and nobody will notice."

Singleton said, "I hope it's not too valuable."

"The publisher will pay." Waldo answered. "Now let's head over to the Brass Helmut and see if we can stir something up."

"This will be exciting," Suzan said, and she took Walling's arm.

But the Brass Helmut was not exciting. It was nearly vacant–a smallish brown rectangle with a bar along the outside edge and only two very elderly fellows on stools near the door. The bartender was a young Latino woman who seemed to recognize Ralph.

"This place smells terrible," Suzan said, loud enough.

"Maybe we're too early," Walling said.

"Look, I can get something going, "Singleton said. "I know I can. If that's what you want."

Waldo answered: "It's not what we want –it's what the venue offers. Don't you get it? We're here just to evaluate what the ambience is."

"Ambience?" Ralph said.

"How fast we get into combat," Walling said.

"The smell is just awful," Suzan said. "Has someone thrown up? I don't think we should stay here."

"We've got to wait the nine minutes," Singleton said, "to make the experiment valid."

"Fuck validity," Waldo shouted. "We're outta here!"

They went out back onto Main Street, past the Beacon pharmacy and on toward some Irish bars further south.

"I really couldn't drink in there. I really couldn't" Suzan said. "I know the experiment won't be valid, and I'm sorry, really sorry about that, but I just couldn't stay there a minute longer. The smell was ghastly, just ghastly."

"No worries, pet, "Waldo answered." The place didn't measure up. That was clear from the minute we entered."

"We didn't give it enough time," Singleton said. "We need to stick to the plan."

"Shut up," Waldo said. "I'm running this operation."

"And I can't really do much walking. It's too cold. I should have brought a heavier coat," Suzan said. "I'm sorry but I can't really walk much more."

"No worries, pet." Waldo said. "We'll go back to the garage and get the van. I've got the best place in mind."

"It's got to have people in it. We're too early," Walling said.

"Maybe," Waldo conceded, "but that can't be helped now. We're launched. Let's get the van."

"We're not thinking clearly," Singleton said. "If we need the van we're going beyond the periphery of our experiment. You can't drive to the toughest bar–that means it could be anyplace.

We're trying to establish the toughest bar in Worcester, a specific place."

"Yes," Suzan said slowly, "a very specific place. With boundaries of possibility."

"Nonsense," Waldo said. "Within the city limits, just too damn far to walk. The van will be okay."

"I don't think so," Singleton insisted.

"You're not being paid to think."

"Are we being paid?" Ralph said.

"One way or another," Waldo said, "now tell him to shut up." Waldo pointed to Singleton, who had taken off his heavy glasses and was rubbing the sides of his nose.

Waldo drove them in the van up Belmont Street to the very edge of Worcester's limits. Then he turned left, went up another hill and parked behind a large house, the first floor of which was labelled, 'Bronzino's Bar.'"

"I've heard of this place," Walling said.

"It's too close to the outskirts, "Singleton said.

"Ralph, tell him to shut up." Waldo said.

Suzan said, "I feel nauseous. Let's stay outside a while, in the cold. That helps. "

"Maybe we should have walked here," Singleton said.

"Walling, where did you find this clown?" Waldo asked.

"How can we measure hostility out there," Walling pointed to Bronzino's, "if we're coming at each other here?"

"We don't need internal antagonism," Suzan, "we certainly don't need that."

"We need a goddamn challenge, so let's go get one," Waldo said, pushing ahead of the group.

3.

Inside Bronzino's, dirty green wall-to-wall carpet gave way to grey linoleum in the expanse of space that must have been living room, dining, room kitchen shotgunned together. There were five round, heavily varnished walnut tables with thick heavily varnished chairs in the space. Three of the tables were filled with patrons–overweight women and men, pitchers of beer, smudged glasses, peanut bowls half empty, shells littering the table tops.

"This could be a Knights of Columbus Bingo party," Waldo said quietly, disappointed.

"I'll get us a pitcher of beer, "Singleton said, as if in expiation. "Sit here." He pulled out a hefty dark chair for Suzan.

"This seems like a family bar," Waldo said, sitting down and apparently irritated that Singleton had taken charge of the next minutes.

"I wonder if there's such a thing as a family bar?" Walling said.

"In London, at the better pubs, you can sit with your family," Suzan said. "Sometimes it so nice to sit with your children in the back garden area of the pub or in a side room away from the noise."

"You have children?" Ralph asked.

"No," Waldo answered. "Only staffers."

"I went with my father to pubs in Highgate and Hampstead. They were lovely." Suzan continued.

"I'm looking at these people and I can't see hostility at all. In fact I'm wondering why I was given the name of this place. It's like a low class, lunch pail bridge convention or something. Strictly lunch pail. And now we have to wait through a pitcher of beer. Probably crappy beer too."

Singleton came back with the beer and six small glasses. He poured a round and said, "Here's to the memory of the Valhalla. Maybe Worcester no longer has a toughest bar."

Waldo countered: "In KL –that's Kuala Lumpur—" he paused looking at Ralph, then added. "That's Malaysia, Kuala Lumpur Malaysia. The capital city. You can't get any bacon. It's a Muslim country. You can't get pork. Course, you can, but only in the Chinese sections of KL. But on the breakfast menus you'll find a reference to 'bacon substitute'. You know what that is?"

Ralph said immediately, "No."

"Well, it's thin strips of veal, strips fried up like bacon. And delicious, but more expensive than bacon."

"Not many things more expensive than bacon lately," Suzan said.

"Right you are, pet. Right you are. This place shows me nothing. Who recommended this place?"

"We've got to finish our beer and wait our nine minutes," Singleton said.

"The hell we do," Waldo said.

"Well, we ought to," Singleton continued. "The experiment has to be fully done and completely replicable."

"I like that word, replicable," Suzan said, savoring the syllables. "Rep lick ah bull."

"In the barracks on Batam Island the workers sleep in hammocks, sometimes four tiers high," Waldo said.

"Tiers?" Ralph asked.

"Tears indeed," Suzan answered. "You should hear him and see his tears over the exploited workers of Batam Island."

"Okay," Waldo said, getting up. "We're outta here."

"I paid for the beer," Singleton said.

"Tell me at the end of the evening," Waldo said.

"Tell you what?"

"How much you shelled out to keep this crew fat and happy."

"We're not so happy," Walling said.

"We're outta here," Waldo said again.

"Maybe we should try some place with Huns around," Singleton suggested.

"Maybe you should wait for your orders," Waldo said.

"Yes!" added Ralph, draining the beer pitcher.

In the van Waldo said, "I've got one more place recommended. On Park Avenue. Maybe a kind of immediate 'post-college' place. Called the Foo Bar."

"I know it," Singleton shouted.

"Oh, he knows it," Waldo echoed. "But I'm worried we're losing our focus. We're not just going to bars. We're trying to find the toughest bar in Worcester. Isn't that what we're trying to do?"

"Who cares?" said Suzan.

"Our readers, pet. The ones who keep us in Bermuda when we need it most."

"Like now," said Walling.

"Oh, not like now," Suzan continued, "certainly not now, when we're collecting all this important data about tough bars in Worcester."

"Yes," said Ralph.

"I like you," Suzan said. "You're affirming."

"One from the scrum is always affirming." Walling said.

The Foo Bar had a dark red glow. The bar stools were filled, but the occupants seemed too well dressed for toughness, and too pre-occupied with the Red Sox game on the two large television screens bracketing the bar. The noise level, however, was promising. Demi shout filled the low ceilinged room and the red lamps with their translucent red shades supplied the proper motivation for fisticuffs.

"We can get something going here," Singleton said, drawing extra chairs to the tiny round table beyond the left end of the bar.

"You've got it backwards and I'm getting tired of pointing that out," Waldo said.

Suzan said, relaxing back into the chair Singleton pushed further under her, "Tell us about Batam Island. You know about the sleeping arrangements."

"Don't get cute," Waldo said. "It's not you."

"Oh, but it's you," Suzan sing-songed back to Waldo.

Walling brought over gin and tonics. "Imagine it's summer," he said.

"Beer and gin doesn't work," Singleton said.

"Let's see," Suzan said. She took a long drink. "Yes, it can work."

Ralph finished his drink in one long swig, and went to the bar to get another.

"Let's go back over the criteria," Waldo said, slumping a bit in his chair, scuffing a bit his Timberlands along the chocolate, stained and worn carpet.

When he got back and before he sat down, Ralph said a bit too loudly, "I hate the Red Sox."

Singleton smiled and nodded at Waldo.

"You've got to remember the criteria." Waldo said.

"If it's not around, you've got to make it happen," Singleton answered.

"The Red Sox suck," Ralph said, again too loudly. A few bar stools spun slowly at the sentiment, turning away from the spring-training, pre-season game.

4.

A distant segment of the bar lifted up and a burly fellow in a grey sweatshirt slowly walked through the opening.

"Here it comes," Singleton said, joyous at the prospect.

He came to within a foot of their table. "You nice people see *Roadhouse* with Patrick Swayze?" the burly fellow asked, taking off his baseball hat and holding it politely with both hands in front of his waist.

"Yes," Walling answered.

"Then you remember Patrick's little suggestion to his bouncers–'be --nice'. So I'm in my Patrick Swayze 'be-nice' phase, just asking you to tone it down. Keep it down, since there happen to be a lot of Red Sox fans here, as you might expect, wouldn't you? Anybody might expect that."

"Yeah, there are dicks everywhere," Ralph said, smiling.

"I'm going to be 'be-nice' and overlook that disappointing observation."

"Up yours," Ralph said.

"I can tell you want me to leave my 'be-nice' persona and become mother-fucking Steven Seagal, is that it?"

"Sure," Ralph answered.

"In *Out for Justice* mother-fucking Seagal puts a cue ball in a handkerchief and slugs teeth all over the pool table. And I like that a lot. All the time he's shouting 'This is your trophy,' holding up his badge. I like that mother-fucking Seagal."

"Hey," Ralph suddenly shouted, "Why don't you curb your foul mouth. Don't you know there's classy cunt here?" He looked at Suzan.

The bar, the game on the television, the announcers in their booths suddenly fell silent at Ralph's proclamation. Red glow grew a notch. Singleton eased up from his chair. The baseball hat fell quietly to the floor. For a very long time, it seemed, no one could think of anything to say, and later Waldo would note the presence of what he called "the very ambivalent pause," the stop-time sequence in which violence or retreat could weigh the balance and flop one way or the other. "That has to be factored in somehow–that moment, the propensity of that moment one way or the other. That's the damn criterion we've been looking for. Some settings, some ambiances stir things one way or another. We've got to break that down, itemize its factors and provide some quantitative measure. That's what we mean by the toughest bar in town."

Ever the deflectionist Walling interceded with an offer, "Here let me pick up your hat." He eased out of his chair, dropped to his haunches and reached for the hat just covering the bouncer's left shoe.

"That's a nice gesture." The fellow said, slowly. "It puts me in the mind of tolerating this asshole," he gestured toward Ralph, who in rising up tossed the table directly at the knees of the bouncer and over Walling's ducking head. The edge of the table cracked directly into the bouncer's kneecaps sounding as if a truck had run over chicken bones. The large center leg of the table drove into Walling's backbone with such force that Walling threw up on the shoes of the bouncer. Not content with this mayhem, Ralph grabbed the bouncer's short hair and slammed his head into the top of the tilted table, not once, not twice, but four machine-gunned times. Teeth spilled out, blood flowed down the table top and into the vomit on the floor. The sound of teeth skittering and Walling gagging , coughing and retching filled the room.

Waldo shouted with delight, "One from the scrum delivers. And how! "

Suzan began taking digital pictures of the cascaded table.

"Jesus!" Singleton said, "Someone call an ambulance. For God's sake call an ambulance."

The young woman behind the bar screamed, "They've killed Eric."

"Not yet," said Ralph. "Not yet, but soon!" He kicked the table over so that it came to rest atop the bouncer's unconscious body, two feet beyond Walling, still kneeling and retching.

"Wait a minute," Waldo shouted. "We're done. It's over. We're done. No more. Nothing more!"

The bar stools emptied as patrons ran for the front door.

"You've killed Eric." The woman insisted again, to the vacant room.

Singleton dragged the table off. "No he's breathing fine, just bloodied. He'll be fine

But, Mr. Jelliffe, I'm not sure how we'll put all this back together."

"Yes, how will we assemble it," Suzan said cheerily. "How does it go back to the way it was?"

"Walling, you okay? " Waldo asked.

"It will take a lot of lawyers to make everything right again," Suzan said, taking more pictures.

"Pet, put away the digital. We need to address the problems at hand," Waldo said evenly.

"Walling, can you speak?"

"Yes, but no wind, no breath."

"Take it easy," Singleton said. "You'll get your breath back. Can you move your arms?"

Walling lifted his arms.

"You'll be fine," Singleton said.

"A whole floor of lawyers," Suzan said. "Maybe more. But maybe we can sue . . . "

"Now you're thinking, Pet. Of course we can sue. How damn aggressive can a bouncer get, coming directly at us? Shouting obscenities. Challenging us. Over some stupid game. Calling us out over some innocent, completely innocent observation aimed at no one. No one at all."

"It smells bad in here," Suzan said.

Waldo said, "Ralph, take Mrs. Jelliffe back to the office and wait there for us. We'll manage everything here, Pet. Don't worry. It'll make a helluva feature."

5.

That night Waldo dreamed of Batam Island. In khaki shorts and mint Teva sandals he walked among the sleeping hammocks of barracks 21-7 and counted for his own collection of possible feature material the rather low number of mosquito nettings surrounding some of the hammocks. The air was dense, mucid, sweat-inducing, so that the polyester of his Guayabera shirt (in

French blue) clung to his back. Waldo thought, "These are my people–young, brown, breathing easily in the hot night." Arms were flung out to him; he had to swivel by several just to reach the far end of the barracks. In the morning they'd each eat a bowl of rice topped by a raw egg. They didn't give a damn about *The Spy,* had no longings for any part of the Worcester Club, envied him nothing of Suzan's largess. Instead, *The Spy* had given him a translator, a wiry forty-year-old with thick black hair somehow knotted in back. In baggy canvas pants and with a lemon colored T shirt the fellow was, Waldo convinced himself, the very personification of Lunch Pail. He promptly dubbed him that and was doubly pleased that the fellow took no insult from the nickname—apparently assumed it was an American term of endearment.

Waldo heard the fellow say from a corner of the barracks, "Captain, what are you doing here?"

"Checking on the troops, LP. Just checking." Waldo answered.

"Checking for what?"

"For conviction, LP, for conviction. I can measure who will get out, who will blossom."

"Blossom?"

"Grow, LP, grow. Enlarge, marry well, acquire, maybe, maybe only acquire."

"Acquire?"

"Buy stuff . . . own stuff. Not flip-flops, LP, but real sandals. Real leather, or maybe real Velcro."

"I know Velcro."

"I'm sure you do, LP. I'm sure you do. It's what keeps us attached, isn't it?"

"Attached?"

"It was a joke, Lunch Pail, just a joke. "

"You're always joking, and I don't like joking. I don't like it. I don't understand it."

"LP, if you can't laugh, you can't live."

"I don't like joking."

"Get over it, Lunch Pail. It makes the world go round."

But LP, drawing closer, had brought up a small mallet from behind him. He tapped it on his palm. Then inverted it so that

II: A, B, C, Lewis Walling

he held the rubber end, the handle extending toward Waldo. He jabbed it into Waldo's chest.

"Hey what are you doing?"

"I don't like joking."

"Good, LP. I understand that."

"I don't like it." He jabbed the handle harder into Waldo, shifted downwards toward his sternum. Then in a savage strike drew back and rammed the end into Waldo's stomach. Waldo doubled over, heard something snap in his lungs, saw a flash camera go off, heard Suzan say, "Oh my! That's not good. That's bad," felt his knees buckle, was aware that the wide boards of the barracks floor had risen strangely to embrace him. LP neatly flipped the handle in his hand so that the mallet end was now in striking position. Waldo cocked his head and presented his left temple for the fatal blow, but woke up before Lunch Pail could bludgeon him. Waldo thought, "God! I love ASEAN."

(Chapter Two)

A week after the tempest at the Foo Bar Lewis Walling went home to New Canaan, Connecticut because his younger sister was celebrating her 18th birthday. He spent most of the drive worrying about that celebration, or more properly the heavy drinking bound to surround the effort. He was certain at some point the buffet at the Wee Burn Club in Darien would be a centerpiece of the event, and that meant Martinis beforehand, wine during and Stingers afterwards, all topped off with what his father called a "rammer"—a final double Martini to force home all the little alcoholic strays into the cage of life in New Canaan. And his sister Janice would be the most obvious drunk in the long room of absolute satiety. He figured he'd have to guide her over the maroon carpet of the Club away from the huge curved windows overlooking the endless brownish greens of the 18 hole golf course, bordering the flagmented, empty patio area with its tables and their collapsed and bound umbrellas–sentinels of proffered booze if you knew the proper number to enter on the tiny pad the waiter offered, but, of course, only when the weather was better.

The buffet was its own reward, Lewis understood, to be savored in recollection and anticipation—especially the overlarge green stuffed olives, "hand massaged," his father always remarked, "by Greek peasants on sun-flecked islands." Shrimp as large as Lewis's third finger curled on the lips of thick crystal dishes filled with fiery scarlet sauce or once, he remembered, not with scarlet but rather orange remoulade —for the start of Lent. A grotesquely large rack of beef ribs, so that he could watch the overlong rounded edge spatula knife work its squirming, swift way through the glistening fiber and out onto his overlarge plate. And everything savored through a Martini haze. "Here you are, Master Lewis," the phony, jovial black chef, Robert, always said lifting a slab onto his plate. "Here YOU are," he repeated with a trace of alarm and menace in his voice, as if he had taken a portion of Lewis's spleen and transferred it onto his plate. Then Robert chuckled quietly, glimpsing into Lewis's startled eyes, as if to say "You're damn right I could gut you like a fish, if I had a mind to, and some proper reward." Instead of rising to that implicit challenge Lewis invariably replied, "Thank you," watching the blood swim across the huge, square plate. He added rice pilaf, roasted broccoli, currant jelly, a few extra shrimp, and, naturally enough, six stuffed green olives.

When he finally got off route 95 and turned into the not quite gated circle of homes in the highest part of New Canaan, Lewis realized it was almost time to meet the train bringing his father home from New York. He's have just enough time to say hello to his mother, if she weren't napping, which he knew she would be, greet the latest servants in the house, a Swiss couple that now occupied what had been his suite above the garage–Susan and Frank, both overweight, accented, strangely formal and apparently ill at ease or menacing in their behavior and wearing too many layers of clothing. He wondered if Janice would be napping too.

But she wasn't. She was at the kitchen booth seated beside Susan and Frank looking through a large white cook book.

Susan said, "Ver looking for ah the best birthday cake for tomorrow. I'm going to make it.

"But I'll help too," Janice added. "You can get Daddy, so Frank can stay here with us."

"Nice to see you, too," Lewis said.

"That's not what I mean. I think you know that."

"Mom up?"

"Not yet," Frank answered. "But shortly."

Lewis noticed there was a tall glass of what might be cream sherry in front of Janice. He remembered a scene in the movie of Fat City: Stacy Keach and Vera Miles at a bar and ordering eight oz. glasses of cream sherry. That was supposedly the bottom of alcoholism.

Cream sherry, or was it Muscatel?

Janice picked up on his noticing and said, "It's just diet Coke. I forgot the ice."

At first he thought it a good defensive joke, but then decided there was an edge of anger in her remark, real offense. It worked well enough, he thought, silencing him. Frank shook his head.

He heard his mother shouting from upstairs. "Someone go and get your father." Her voice sounded tired and muffled by the swinging door to the dining room.

2.

As always his father came jauntily out from the tiny colonial station, on to the asphalt that led across the road to the parking lot. As always, Lewis parked back-in so that he stood now outside the car. His father liked to make a clean getaway, ahead of the exiting traffic, shouting "Let's go," as he got into the Buick Lewis had swapped for his dusty Toyota. "You just get home?"

"No. A while ago."

"And they made you come here right off?"

"I didn't mind."

"Well, take Ridgefield. Let's avoid downtown, unless you want to refresh your memory."

"I don't."

"Neither do I. And there's nothing new to see. Your mother up?"

"Getting there."

"Good. Susan and Frank are good for her."

Did that mean Janice wasn't? Rather than explore that thought, Once on Ridgefield, with overarching trees forming an arcade out of New Canaan , Lewis said, "I was in a bar fight in Worcester."

"In one, or saw one?"

"Kinda in one. A fellow at my table slugged the bouncer. It was pretty scary. The table fell on me."

"You were under the table?"

"Yes, but because I was trying to pick something up."

"Maybe it's better to stay under the table."

"Not when it falls on you. I threw up."

"What were you drinking?"

Lewis regretted getting into details. "Beer."

"It took rum to get me puking, when I was your age."

"I'm worried about the legal stuff."

"Did someone get hurt?"

"Maybe the bouncer got a concussion."

"I wonder how you'd tell," his father said, chuckling.

"Unfortunately I don't think it's much of a joke."

"Well I wouldn't worry about it, until you get subpoenaed."

Lewis thought that, indeed, was his father's genius–the ability not to think about things until a decision demanded thought. It must have freed him up for all sorts of activities everyone else had no time for. It was a highly cultivated art of dismissal, utterly un-reflected on, until converging forces dictated choosing. It seemed he could slick the un-immediate back as he slicked his long hair straight back from his long forehead. Tall and immaculately tailored he often struck Lewis as a model business man stepping out from a magazine spread. Daily cufflinks, almost unimaginable in Lewis's mind. They clicked on the steering wheel as his father turned to him and said quickly–having decided apparently even more quickly, "I'll mention it to Jack, and see if he thinks any steps need to be taken." The car glided into the deepening hill lanes of New Canaan.

Lewis thought, steps to what? And then he remembered the bar altercation. So his father had been mulling it over despite the quick dismissal. Lewis felt better— as if he did actually matter. And better yet, Jack would handle it. "Thanks," he said with relief emphasizing the sentiment.

"You don't think I'd let you burn in hell, do you?"

"Thanks."

"Not in hell, but maybe in the Worcester County jail . . . " his father said laughing.

"Please, not that."

"Yes," his father said, "not that."

When they got back to the house Frank had a tall bourbon and water waiting. "The Mrs. is getting dressed," he said.

"Dinner in forty- five minutes," Susan added. "Roast lamb."

"Hi Daddy," Janice said, tilting her cream sherry toward them.

His father nodded, took the bourbon and hurried out of the kitchen and upstairs.

Sighing visibly Janice said, "See, he does care. .. . Just not much."

"He's got my legal problems to worry about," Lewis added.

"I wish I had legal problems," Janice continued, with a slight laugh.

"Well, work at it." Lewis said. "And meanwhile let's let them get to work too." Lewis motioned toward Susan and Frank. He took Janice's hand and led her through the swinging door out of the dining room and into the pine paneled library.

When Janice had settled on the daybed, sheathed in blue felt fabric, she said, "Father Fay is coming to dinner, aren't you thrilled?"

"To tend to our wayward souls," Lewis said.

"Of course, and to make Daddy a convert."

"I doubt that," Lewis said watching a tiny chipmunk slowly, carefully, knead its way across the immense blue tarp over the swimming pool in the backyard.

-§-

At Serena B says, "Pretty leisurely chapter and not enough on Lewis, much less on the wondrous Annie May. And who gives a dam about Waldo and LP? Am I supposed to feel sympathy for the peasants working at the dealership, or the Iranian mechanics? Oh, excuse me! I meant to say the Iranian 'technicians' every one of them fucking illegal and, and smart. Techs."

"Waldo and Suzanne are important in the evolution of things," C says, smiling.

"And LP?" A asks.

"I'm thinking of having him kill Waldo," C answers.

"Jesus!" B says, "Just a spoiler or maybe a nifty narrative hook. Grow up. I thought it was Lewis's story."

"But," A says, "Lewis is dead. Do you want the ghost of Lewis, is that it? I'm more interested in this Father Fay, spelled with an 'a' and not, surprisingly, and more appropriately, with an 'e.'"

"So why not start here with the second chapter of the Waldo-LP saga?"

-§-

(Chapter Two.Two)

Hands resting on the rope belt over a protuberant stomach Father Fay stood by the fireplace. His reddish face, freckled and jowly was capped off by a neat, combed-down pad of hair that in its precise lines seemed almost painted on his skull. Lewis wondered if in fact the priest wore a toupee. It seemed only a screwdriver could pry under that arranged hair, or that permanent, faintly mocking smile. Lewis envied the priest's certitude–that smug sense that he grasped the complexities of the world, surmounted them, and had moved into contemplative majesty alone above all else. There he was, God's emissary at the very far end of a magnificently buffed hallway, halfway to the moon, beckoning you toward him, toward his wisdom and all-collapsing embrace of love, his sureness rolling down toward you over the glistening marble or linoleum or maybe heavily polyurethaned wood.

"So you've run amuck with the authorities," he said to Lewis. He paused, adjusting the rope belt by sliding it a bit to his left. "Ah, you're surprised at my information. But if you think about it, I'm sure you'll conclude your father's concern has been shared." The priest took a long, indulgent swallow of the iceless bourbon in his overlarge high ball glass.

"Oh, you two aren't dredging up all that unpleasantness in Worcester are you? Surely we've better things to discuss. Besides, it's over and done with it, isn't it Louie?" his mother said

From her perch on the daybed next to the fireplace.

"Well, there is still a hearing," Lewis said.

"I'll make a novena, and your father probably already has, and with less distant authorities."

Father Fay chuckled. "One nice thing about judicial authorities in Massachusetts–when they don't conspire, they traffic, and their trade is most responsive to currency."

"Of which the Vatican has an amplitude," Lewis's father said entering the room.

"Alas, not for secular investment," Father Fay said.

Lewis's mother held up her empty drink glass and motioned to her son. "Be a dear and touch me again, and find your sister–she needs to put in an appearance here before dinner. And not another word about legalities. That's what lawyers are for, aren't they Daddy?"

"When you pay them, my dear. Only when you pay them." He said, sitting down in the huge pine armchair across from the daybed. He set his tall bourbon on the wide level arm . . .

The Riches of This World, Part B

(Spleenectomy – A Play in One Act)

The curtain opens to reveal a traditional knotty pine library (sans any book shelves) with two blue felt couches with plaid skirts, and brilliantly red bolsters. One couch resides beneath eight framed windows running the full width of the room, overlooking a wooded area. Stage left front there is a brick chimney with presumably an angled fireplace not visible to the audience. To the right of the couch beneath the windows is a massive pine arm chair with wide flat arms sufficient to hold a pitcher of martinis or iced tea. Hunched over in front of the fireplace is an elderly overweight woman in a long dress and heavy cardigan sweater. Abutting that fireplace is the second couch and on it sits a young woman, perhaps 18 years old, with her legs tucked up under her. She holds a slightly oversize high ball glass full of bourbon. Standing beside her with his right knee abutting the couch is an overweight Catholic priest in cassock and collar.

Sitting on the couch beneath the windows is a woman of 50 in a bright blue (almost electric blue) pant suit. She is holding a highball glass with three ice cubes and a clear liquid visible to the audience. Entering from stage right is her husband of 55 years wearing a brown nicely tailored suit and he too, is carrying a highball glass full of dark liquid.

The standing old woman says perhaps a little too loudly, "Sonny can you put another log on the fire?"

The seated woman, Estelle, answers, "Gram, Louie's upstairs and he can't hear you."

Abruptly the priest turns and walks to the room's entrance (stage right) and shouts "Lewis! Lewis! More wood for the fire."

Gram: "My nose. My nose. It gets so cold. Louie knows that."

Estelle: (Derisively) "Oh father! You'll wake the dead, indeed the whole household."

Priest: "Only Lewis, my dear. Only Lewis. And long since he should have been roused from embarrassing slumber."

Entering husband to Estelle: "I couldn't have done the shouting better—"

Estelle: "Well, Daddy, in that case—"

Dad: "But in fact. Lewis is in the kitchen with Annie May, doing his homework. So, Gram let me stoke up the fire."

Estelle: "Don't dirty your suit, dear."

Husband: "That's what the carrying case is for."

Priest: "Mr. Walling, let me take care of that. A cassock is eminently washable."

Estelle: "Janice, you see how Father Fay is always helping. Seems as if you might follow that example and help Lewis with his homework. It would have the added benefit of freeing Annie May for her real duties."

Janice: "Of course." Slowly getting off the couch as the priest tosses a massive log on the fire and pokes at it with a wrought iron poker, increasing light in the room. Husband sits in the pine chair and sets his drink on the wide left armature.

Estelle to Janice: "Seems you couldn't be moving more slowly. I'm sure your affection for Lewis is stronger than that."

Priest: "It's his homework that slows her, I'd suggest. She's reluctant to take over that task for him."

Estelle: "I'm not sure you truly grasp family life."

Priest: "Ah touché. I believe I'll have another bourbon."

Estelle: "Send Annie May in, Janice when you get to the kitchen."

Janice: "Of course."

Estelle: "You may have to wait a while, Father. But Annie May will come, I'm positive of that. Just as Mom will get her nose finally warmed up."

Priest: "Mine is a waiting and a serving profession."

Estelle: "Such charming self-deprecation. We all need to emulate it."

Husband: "Did I read that Louie Budenz now teaches at Fordham, of all places. Could that be true?"

Priest: "Yes indeed. I suspect Bishop Sheen got him that post as well as his new found faith. He was always a Catholic, but lost his way."

Husband: "I should say."

Priest: "As you have indeed. This Bishop has done God's work resoundingly. Taking one of the greatest of lost souls back to the Lord, to Holy Church."(He holds out his empty glass to the young black woman appearing at stage right, and then continues:) "Fulton J. knows intimately how to appeal to Communists—what levers of social action he can press to get astonishing results. Ah, Annie May can you summon my beloved acolyte, perhaps bringing me my drink? That would be splendid. All blessings." (Calling after her, since she has turned back leaving the stage).

Husband: "The Monsignor is a bit of the caped crusader, don't you think, in that crinkling cassock and sweeping jacket."

Priest: "Jesuits have always been a bit swishy. But a powerful voice and presence."

Estelle: "He's really wonderful. Captivating. Rooting traitors out of our government."

Lewis enters the room, a boy of perhaps 12 years.

Priest: "Ah Louie with my drink. Here, boy, let me give you a hug." They embrace for perhaps a second too long.

Estelle: "And where is Janice?"

Lewis: "I think she went to her room."

Estelle: "Well, you just sprint upstairs after her and tell her to come back down. We haven't concluded drinks with Father Fay.

Don't let her be so rude." Lewis breaks off from the priest and exits. "I'm so sorry Father my children seem to forget their manners."

Priest: "That's their natural destiny."

Estelle: "Hardly. I've taught them better than that. They know better than that. They'll be right here soon enough. In the meantime tell me whether you actually ever met Bishop Sheen. I'd love to hear about that."

Priest: "Never, but once in Westport I was at a party where, allegedly, he'd been there earlier. It was in an all glass house on the lushest green lawn."

Estelle: "Gram! Don't get so close to the fire. You'll go up in flames."

Gram: "Not much danger in that. I'm too old and soggy."

Estelle: "Your clothes could burn, and the soot would ruin our new rug." Laughs.

Scene ends in sudden darkness.

Scene 2

Estelle having aged some thirty years stands in her bright blue pant suit before an immense closed double door painted iridescent yellow. She is alone on stage staring up at the doors which are slightly over 12 feet high. A sputtering micro-phoned voice repeats at two minute intervals:

"Doors to the ICU will open in five minutes. Your visit cannot exceed ten minutes. You must exit the unit when that ten minutes is up. Make sure you are gowned, masked and shoe-protected before entrance."

Estelle quickly but awkwardly gets into her shoe protections, gown and face mask. As Estelle struggles getting properly dressed, the electronic voice repeats the message: "Doors to the ICU will open in three minutes. Your visit cannot exceed ten minutes. You must exit the unit when that ten minutes is up. Make sure you are gowned, masked, and shoe-protected before entrance."

As Estelle waits, she adjusts her shoe-boots, retying them and then five red lights overhead blink and the dual enormous doors open outward folding back on themselves, revealing a series of beds and patients mounted so that they appear arranged for viewing from back stage to front elevated in ways the audience can watch each. Moreover there is a second tier above what might be mid curtain of the stage. On this tier again slightly slanted for audience view is Lewis's father, thinner and white shrouded with an IV unit close by releasing clear liquid into his left arm. He appears to be sleeping. As the twin doors fold back there is an escalation of sound, clattering, grinding, whining, clicking as if a myriad electronic medical devices are all functioning at once.

As the doors fold back, entering from stage right is a woman of about 30 years in a long white blouse and dark trousers and sneaker shoes encased in required clear plastic, but the woman is not wearing a gown or mask or hat. She strides swiftly to the side of the man at center on a crankable bed, her father.

Estelle: "Janice! How did you get in? What are you doing here? You're not dressed properly. You could be dangerous to him, don't you see that? Your dress is incorrect."

Janice: "I thought you'd be upset by my dress. You were never in favor of casual even if elegant, were you?" (laughs) "So stay put. Don't upset the scene. I've come to say a few things to Daddy. I hope he can hear, still hear."

Estelle: "Don't you dare! Your father deserves sleep, quietude, deep sleep. It's what he needs."

Janice: "Bull shit. It's what you need. Always what you need. That, always, comes first, doesn't it? Well, it ain't so now, dearie. Not so now. I'll have my say. What he needs to hear, is what he needs to hear. He has to be held accountable, doesn't he? Of course he does. The record needs to be laid out. To be set down. To be ENUNCIATED. I intend to do just that, and you can't stop me even if you could fly up here—which I imagine you could, under some circumstances, actually do. But you can't save him from the truth. Jesus, the truth never counted for anything in your sorry life, but before he ends his sorry life, he'll hear the truth. Actually hear it and know exactly what he's done. What he can't deny. What you can't deny, although, God knows, you'd deny everything and anything that threatens your sick arrangement of reality. That sweet, swimming fantasy you live. Jesus! Don't fly up here. Don't you dare! I've got a machete for you, you know. Better not fly up here. Better you'd just kneel down and beg forgiveness for your sorry life, for the sorry way you've fucked up every one of us. You and the monster here. Oh he'll have to listen now won't he? He'll have to hear me, see me and recognize what he did. The whole sick recitation."

Estelle: "He did nothing! Nothing. You know that. You can't think that, can you? Listen to your soul. It's crying out for the real truth. You know that in your heart of hearts don't you. You were such a sweet, loving child. You've always had the sweetest disposition. Listen to that goodness in you. It's so there, so full, so radiant. This blackness, this hatred, it's not you. You've been taken over, assumed the very bodily shape of Pearl Button. You don't want that. No one does. No child of mine could ever embrace such sickness. Let that natural sweetness out . . . let it now! Your father resonates to it. You can cure him, or if not cure, then call him back from the abyss, the chasm of your accusations. How could you? He was always the sweetest of men, full of concern, radiant in his concern for you. How could you?

Janice: Why don't you shut up! Filling the air with your sour yearning. Sour yearning and carefully dismantling of your very offspring. He'll know I know and can remember, even if he can't or won't. What he did, how he did it. How he maneuvered it, groomed me for it. The sweet love you sigh about, laced with his sticky fingers stuck in my body. Stuck deep in my body. And for what? Some secret sick pleasure!

Estelle: How can you talk like this? What happened to you? Where did you walk out of sweetness, the loveliness you were as a child, the sweet compliant loveliness? And now look at you. Look at how you dress now. How hollowed out you are. How can you be doing this to me? Look at how you dress.

Scene 3

The curtain has dropped and suddenly from stage right emerges a figure in a satin maroon/pink cape, a huge silver cross dangling over his elaborately shirted white vestments. He has gleaming, lucite-covered black shoes, sparkling in the single spot aimed on him. He strides slowly, majestically to center stage and smiling broadly addresses the audience.

Monsig: "Yes, yes, you might marvel at the clothing Monsignor's wears. Once when I was talking at an elementary school—something lately I no longer and sorrowfully don't do, I made the terrible mistake of asking one inquisitive girl who actually stood up to observe me, 'and what do you see?' She answered quickly and easily and I suppose obviously, 'I see Cock Robin!' Someone should write a long treatise on the clothes of Monsignors, Bishops and Archbishops, perfect for a coffee table somewhere in Hades, perhaps." Smiling indulgent look to the audience.

"I'm afraid some of you may have heard these remarks on Satan and sin before—dismissing them then, as you do now, as only the bleatings of one worn-out lamb on the shoulders of his Lord clamoring for your spare attention. I'm afraid I do repeat myself, harping on the truth, perhaps . . . Which reminds of a Physics professor of mine who made a career of giving the same supercharged speech over and over at various venues, after he had won some venerable prize and international recognition. He gave the speech so often and at the bequest and financing of so many agencies that he regularly employed a chauffeur to drive him from one place to the next. And after nearly of year of such barnstorming (though that is too slick, too full a term for what was going on in those hour-long lectures), the chauffeur observed casually enough, 'I've heard your speech so often I could recite it faultlessly—perhaps even improving on your delivery.' The professor took up the challenge (he'd been doing so all his life). And he said, 'Okay in the next auditorium let's exchange suits and you deliver the speech. I'll sit in the audience as your chauffeur.' And that's what they did and the chauffeur manqué professor faultlessly delivered the lecture in a way convincing even the most skeptical in the audience. But at the end a fellow stood up in the side balcony and said, 'Impressive performance, Professor, but can you elaborate on why E=mc2 comes directly out of the reaction you have so meticulously described?'

The faux professor seemed momentarily stunned but quickly recovered by saying in ever louder tones:

'That's a very broad but ultimately stupid question, but easily answered. So easily in fact that I'm going to ask my chauffeur to stand and answer it.'

The Monsignor paused admiring the laughter growing toward applause then said, "So, sitting out there somewhere is our chauffeur willing to untangle our darkest thoughts about Satan and sin. Let's listen to him."

"He says there are three points to be made: 1. The human soul's natural residue is viciousness. 2. The rational scaffolding above this residue radiates compassion. 3. The regulating mechanism between viciousness and compassion gyrates wildly. Ah, you're thinking 'Good days and bad.' Or perhaps you're thinking God's grace regulates the gyration. Or maybe faith does. Or religious commandments. Or Canon Law. But our faith-filled or faith-emptied chauffeur veers away from such assertions. Rather, he argues that national culture throttles all gyrations. Thus the good Japanese hearing only two inner voices one commanding 'butcher' and the other 'salve,' listens to that unconscious directive of culture which asks only that social expectations provide guidance: what do my neighbors suggest or sanction? The good American prefers to consult his gut which gravitates naturally toward violence and provides soothing only in anger. Butchery ensues . . . Would another joke help? Here's one with a religious and possibly raunchy (depending on your personal extent of moral or is it only morale disease):

The pope is flying from Mexico City back to Rome, and in his papal first class seat he is solving a cross word puzzle. Anon, he asks the fellow sitting across from his very wide aisle, "Do you happen to know a four-letter word for woman ending in 'unt'? The fellow is visibly shocked and struggles for an answer. At the last possible moment he realizes there is a way out of his embarrassment, and he rushes to say, "Yes I get it. Of course it's 'Aunt'. The Holy Father sighs and asks, "Do you have an eraser?"

"By now the chauffeur is not much welcome as an explicator. But he pushes on in his best prophetic mode. He shouts that it is necessary to at least toy with the notion of national culture proving to be the ultra-determinant. And he continues: —in the modern world everything about American culture springs from a single date, August 6, 1945 at 8:15 a.m. the dropping of the first atomic bomb on the city of Hiroshima, Japan. That event destroyed the boundaries Americans unconsciously believed between military and civilian targets, between just and unjust war, between good and evil itself, and thus freed the natural American soul to deal its mephitic medicine upon humanity. D.H. Lawrence argued the original American was a savage, a natural killer. And without the conditioning of remembered history, long history, the American gravitates naturally to his instinctive viciousness—witless killing on a scale appropriate to the excesses of the 20th century. How might that be stemmed? Redirected? Or more accurately how might the forces that called such savagery into fruition be otherwise propitiated? What might be the context that would soften, shrink, stultify the natural tendency toward butchery? Why is warning never sufficient? Why does exhortation always fail? What are viable alternative paths, alternative techniques? They always begin with a narrative, a story. Let me tell you one:

"When she first came under my guidance it was through an aleatory coincidence. I had attended a lovely garden party in southeast Connecticut and a priest at the local diocese (incidentally a priest I had been instructed to mentor) told me about her case. She came from a fairly well to do family, apparently stable, apparently normal, yet she had sunk into depression and medication and alcoholism. The good cleric had been ineffective in righting things. We perhaps expect too much of our priests—more often than not they are chauffeurs in elevated garb. Naturally I asked to see her. And she came to me in New York later that spring. I think she was delighted to say she was seeing a Monsignor in New York City. I've noticed that is something of a chip in the game in southeastern Connecticut's Catholic community, though perhaps not in God's enterprise." He smiles saturninely at the audience. "When I asked how she was doing, she immediately began weeping, more than weeping, sobbing. But I sensed there was a certain theatricality to her uncontrol, masking something and so I suggested something I had never done before and never since, I suggested we immediately begin guided imagery— a technique quite out of favor now for reasons that will become clear. She nodded consent and seemed bolstered by my willingness to begin treatment without any preliminary exploration. Of course that was not really the case. I had reviewed with her priest a sweet little man, given a bit overmuch to the Lord's love of wine." A shallow laugh. "I asked her to close her eyes and immediately I re-commenced the music I had been listening to earlier during my usual morning meditation, Bach's wondrous cantata #180. And following the textbook procedure of that time, I weakly, faintly, sweetly suggested that she regress in time to her early childhood, perhaps by envisioning the room she spent most of her time in during her years, say, from 4 to 7. I asked her to describe the room—it had apparently vertical blue lined wallpaper —blue lines like bars on an all-white wall. It occurred to me at the time (and was borne out later) that the chamber seemed like confinement, perhaps a prison cell. What was it like in that room, I asked and she didn't answer, merely rocked slightly in the soft chair she was sitting. Is it a pleasant memory? I asked. Again she didn't answer but began a soft mewling sound, very faint at first, then swelling a bit, then fading again. What are you feeling in that room? There was a certain throb to Bach's incredible music, as the chorale opening proceeded: *Deck thyself, o soul beloved,/ Leave sin's dark and murky hollows,/ Come, the brilliant light approaching,/Now begin to shine with glory;/* What are you feeling in that room? I asked again. Then I heard her sighing, 'Daddy, ooth ooth,' but the music suddenly broke into a lively ingratiating tune, threatening the mood, so that she seemed to be emerging from a disturbing memory. I hastily pushed the repeat button and the chorale recommenced, slipping her back to whatever wilderness that had been identified and temporarily lost. She coasted through the first verses again and fixed on the concluding sentiments: *For the Lord with health and blessing/Hath thee as his guest invited./ He, of heaven now the master./ Seeks his lodging here within thee./* 'Daddy, why stop now?' She sighed with utmost clarity. 'Why stop now?' There was a terrible childish curiosity in her question and she turned to me, eyes open, staring into mine, as if I could answer her question, as if I was the perpetrator of whatever it was that she didn't want to stop. I was stricken with the feeling that I had made a terrible, fundamental and sickening mistake. I had played carelessly with something that needed far more thought, far more consideration, far more planning and consideration. I realized that through some stupid arrogance I had taken her to places neither of us were prepared to deal with in any healing fashion. I let Bach's recitative work its frolic summon her ability to carry on as if nothing had been unearthed, no residue re-sifted. Her eyes brightened and she smiled widely and made a move to stand up. Don't stand I commanded her with rather more sharpness than I expected. I was frightened she would lose her balance, as I had lost mine. She slumped back. 'Why,' she asked, 'are you afraid I'd attack you.' No. Rather, the very opposite I found myself saying—more than alarmed at my own expression. Once again Bach's music rescued me. Suddenly the next recitative intruded on the liveliness so I followed along as the soprano intoned, *My heart within feels fear and gladness;/It is with fear inspired/When it that majesty doth weigh,/When it no way into the secret findeth,/Nor with the mind this lofty work can fathom./ God's Spirit, though, can through his word instruct us/How here all spirits shall be nurtured/ Which have themselves in faith arrayed.*

-§-

But suddenly B interrupts his reading and later at Serena says, "I stopped plowing through the play, because it got off the track. Really derailed with the Monsignor. Who cares about the Monsignor? I wanted information about Lewis, about his upbringing, about his decision to join the Army, about his exit from Annie May. Haven't you got something about that? Give us the backstory. Good Christ, don't burden us with your feelings about the Catholic Church. Or Janice's lurid imaginings."

A answers, "He doesn't care about the church. Only that sick family does."

"I'm not buying it. You know the Japanese really got it right. Every fiction is just an I-narrative." B says.

"Fiction is fiction. Imagination is real," A answers. "You need to accept imagination's liberation. Really, you do. And of course some red wine."

"The fact is I'm bored with the play. Give me something else. To tell the truth your 'play' makes me lonesome for something chapter-like on Lewis's unhappiness, or maybe Janice's derangement."

"Okay. Okay. No problem. Just suffer through another scene or two." C says quietly.

"Fuck you," B replies.

Scene 4: Back in the ICU unit.

Janice is at her father's bedside on the elevated section of the set. Below on the stage down front a priest walks to center stage and from the opposite side a physician in white lab coat joins him.

Physician: "I'm glad to see you here. It's reassuring to me, because before I enter the OR I always pause and ask God to guide my hands."

Priest: (evidently Father Fay from Scene 1) "And from what I hear the Lord guides them splendidly."

Physician: "It's true most days I am aware of some power steering the scalpel. One feels God in such extreme circumstances, don't you agree?"

Priest: — Of course! But I worry whether the cutting has much to do with the healing.

Physician: —Well, I can remove the swollen spleen, but I can't cut away the disease. That's relentless. I remove the evidence, but the crime continues.

Priest: —So you are the elongator of the Lord's relished ravaging? Carnage!

Physician: — You're not much into solace, are you father?

Priest: —Not much, but surely I would not impede your cutting. The Lord bless your skilled hands, and your proud heart.

Abruptly the scene darkens and a spot light opens on Janice and her father's bed above the departing Priest and Physician.

Janice: —After years of saying nothing, enduring everything and saying nothing, I've come here to acknowledge what we never speak of. Do you hear me, Daddy? Do you? I know what you did to me, what your smelly fingers stroked their way into me. Through my pathetic and vulnerable body. My sick and exploited body. I can feel you still, your slobbering, blubbering presence. Dead drunk and groping, gathering me up in your sick fantasies. And now I can't even listen to your denials. You cannot speak. Struck dumb by some crude justice for your sick nature. Impotent now, utterly helpless so that you have to listen to what I'm saying. You never wanted to do that, did you? You couldn't. To do it you'd have

to acknowledge someone beyond your sick needs, your desperation. Absolute desperation. If I could only have struck you dumb
and paralyzed years ago, rendered you stunned in your depravity.
Utter depravity. I couldn't see it then, only then endured it. So I
come now to lay it before you, put it on your inert heart, ladle it on
your sick soul. Pour back into you the bloody semen gravy of your
diseased lust. Ladle that thick gravy over and into and beyond
your occasionally fiercely closed eyes. Marlene says you should be
locked up. Locked up? Can you see yourself as locked up? I can
see you there.

-§-

At Serena's B says, after sucking Japanese-style on his buttered angel hair spaghetti, "Don't you think you're laying it on a bit thick
here? Rhetoric can't accomplish, especially in the setting you've
chosen what some precise stage business might better convey. Say,
why not have Janice take his limp hand and thrash it around her
crotch? Why wouldn't that work? It would be more powerful than
the speech you give her. I say lay off the language and let stage
business work its magic. What do you think?"

A says, "I don't think you're serious. Only trying to score
points off our hapless author. I'd like to hear more from the
Monsignor."

"Jesus," B remarks, sighing. "Enough is enough."

-§-

Scene 4. Continued:

Suddenly from upper stage left a tall, overweight woman in tight
jeans and a tan blazer over a black blouse strides quickly toward
the bed holding Daddy. She is clapping her hands apparently ap-
plauding Janice's previous speech. It's Marlene.

Marlene—Even if he can't hear, won't hear it, it's a great truth
and what a step forward for you, Janny. Doesn't it lift your soul,
free you in surprising ways? Oh yes it does! And he couldn't stand

that. That's why he's silent. But I guarantee he's hearing all of it, scrambling for safer ground—looking for his darling wife-rescuer to take him to safe, booze-soaked ground. Oh yeah, let it out sister. Let it out. Together we can cut his heart out and leave it on the tarmac of self-hate. Let it out. Shape it into a stiletto of revenge—healing hatred. Come on, gal, you're just getting started. Brace yourself. Open the Bombay. Open the Bombay. That scummy piece of shit needs to get all the pellets of his corruption dropped on his slimy soul. Shit on him! Shit, shit, shit on him. (She hugs Janice from behind, clamps her wrists and guides her hands toward Daddy's throat). Let's tear his larynx out. I'll help you digging your fingers in. Claw away, Claw away, it's so good for you. So deliciously good.

Estelle enters running from upper stage right. She grabs, clamps on Marlene's hair and yanks her back off of Janice and eventually toward the floor. Janice instantly releases her father's neck and sobbing screams, "Daddy. Daddy! I'm so sorry. She made me do it.. I couldn't have done it.

Estelle: Of course you couldn't have done it. She made you do it. Why oh why does she have the Indian sign on you?

Abruptly the curtain drops and from a wing emerges once again, the Monsignor gliding as if on casters to center stage.

Monsig: An interesting word 'The Indian Sign,' Might it stand in for every perception of the basic evil swirling through us? I do suppose it reflects the American fear and shame concerning their original forebearers. But no matter the label exempts us from judgment—hapless victims all. All corruption is always out there.

Monsignor gestures to his audience.—Out there but awaiting redemption, yes, so panting for redemption. I know your thirst . . .

From an unseen audience member: —Up your gigi with a wa-wa brush!

Monsig: Dear child, language slander is no salvation. None what so ever. I know your dispossession, your separation and your fear. I know it. Is what you hear tremulous? Is it? Oh no! It is the happy sunshine of certitude! Come in from fear and loneliness. Come home to the grandeur of God. Be charged by it. Lurch to embrace it. Surrender to grace. Let its shudders fill your body.

Listen to my voice. I echo the Lord's word, his salving/saving grace. Let the Holy Spirit reign now. Now. Now. At once!

Scene 5.

At night and updrawn curtain reveals a very dark room, with walls in blue and white stripes about one inch wide, rising perpendicular from a dark blue carpet. Gradually a black woman in a wicker rocking chair, stage left, is revealed. And there is a double bunk bed, with a sobbing 12 year old boy on the bottom bunk. The rhythmic sound of the gentle rocking seems to grow louder through, apparently a sound system of some kind, and the boy's sobbing seems to flow along with that increasing noise. Just as the racket reaches a level to seem to become something else, it stops. And the woman speaks.

Annie May: Louie you were doing good, you were winning. There was no reason to stop. You done good. You stopped her good. There was no reason, none at all. So why are you crying? You had her down. Everyone saw that. Even Griffin saw that. He stopped talking 'bout you. He stopped. It all stopped. You won. You won, silly boy. You won. So there's nothing to cry about.

Lewis: (barely audible) It was all so stupid. (sobbing) Stupid. Pointless. I didn't want to. I didn't.

Annie May: Of course you didn't. You're good, Louis. You're so good. They're the bad ones. All of 'em. All of them. You don't have to cry. You did nothing wrong. Nothing. And they knew it. That's why they slinked away. You notice how they slinked away? Leaving you setting on her and alone sitting on her. So why you crying? Nothing to cry about. Nothing. So let's get up and go fix some popcorn and sit a spell in the kitchen. How about that?

Lewis: I could have hurt her, but I didn't want to. I really didn't. It was all so stupid.

Annie May: You could have lambasted her. She knew that. They knew that. That's why they slinked away. You done nothing wrong. So let's go get some popcorn. We can use the air popper. I like the way it rings. We can make some popcorn and we can melt the butter on the pan above where the corn comes out. You remember that don't you? Like artillery fire you said. Corn just popping out and the butter melting in the aluminum tray and pops going off everywhere.

Lewis: Like artillery fire. Yes.

Annie May: Yes. So you can get up and we can go into the kitchen and we can have a good time, watching the popping. Can't we?

Lewis: (rising a little and then flopping back down on the lower bunk) Oh, I don't know. I don't know. It was all so stupid. I'm not what they wanted, what everybody wanted. I want to be free of being wanted to do something, anything, everything. I just wanted to crawl away. And I couldn't do that, at least until you pulled me off her. Jesus, you're strong. You pulled me right up. I didn't know how to get up.

And then there was no sense in even trying to get up. I was disassembled in dirty water with life swimming away with my intestines, un-lassoed by blood. Seeping away . . . seeping away.

Scene 6.

Fulton: to Father Fay: You've told me Lewis's mother used the phrase, "Indian sign" as a way of judging his attachments. If he played tennis too often or too furiously, too competitively she noted that by saying, "It has the Indian sign on you." If he had a close friend she wondered if that person had the "indian sign" on Lewis. So that eventually even the suggestion of "indian sign" on an event, friend, attachment of any kind rinsed the entity in sour rejection. Life at its peak, he initially believed, was always free of such "indian sign" significance, but eventually he came to understand than any real commitment was subject to such dismissal. If he believed anything, sought any real conviction, that only was evidence of the "Indian Sign" taking over his mind, his brain, his essence. And as such it must be rejected.

But there was a tandem to that stress, and alternative that she floated effortlessly and continuously. The Indian Sign naturally propelled him into a person he wasn't, a phony errant figure that she effortlessly and continuously fashioned, named, "Pearl Button." Forcing him into an alternative version of himself which she tirelessly called "Pearl Button." The phrase was the perfect complement to his dissolving persona. "That wasn't you, that was Pearl Button," she said in disavowal of some action he'd undertaken, some thought he had that didn't envelope into her categories of acceptability. Have I caught your grasp of his situation? Little Pearl Button had disgusting thoughts of autonomy, independence, self-sufficiency, and what were such thoughts, only Indian Signs of unacceptability. Such unacceptability induced automatically, rigorously, abandonment, withdrawal of any love. Have I caught the essence of what you think was going on in poor Lewis's upbringing?

Fay: Almost magically, with precision beyond my feeble appreciation.

Fulton: Put the spatula down. Such frosting is unbecoming, and doubtless will spot my crimson garments. (laughs). So you're proposing a bifurcated personality, is that it? Indian signed Lewis cast into Pearl Button's stunned opprobrium? And most ominously that wounded lad attracted the sad Pearl Button of yourself—that Pearl Button the Bishop chastised and instructed you to take my counseling?

Fay: Yes and how can I counsel the lad?

Fulton: Why counsel? Aren't we all caught between Satanic thirst and our muffled, charitable and sensual longings? Isn't that the normal situation to be sorted out or not according to God's grace?

Fay: God created "Pearl Button?"

Fulton: If not created, then allowed to emerge. The lurking presence in the sinews of our better selves. Aging is the agent of suppressions, isn't it? So that we might overcome our deficiencies. For example in your case—better for you to meditate on your obsessions with his "counsel". Has he got the "indian sign" on you, good brother?

Fay: Monsignor, I beg forgiveness now and at the hour of my death.

Fulton: More than forgiveness (already easily given and accepted), but rather redirection toward Janice's whose collapse before her own "indian signed Pearl Button," will prove fatal barring your intervention. Isn't it so?

Fay: [musingly] Isn't it so? Isn't it so? Janice is more than I can cope with. Nothing good will come of it. I'd prefer to turn our attention to Annie May, the one chance Lewis might have had to find himself among the Pearl Buttons so Indian-signed to extinction.

-§-

"Food for another luncheon, "B interrupted. "Jesus! I can't stand such prelate-analysis billowing around your empty plate presentation."

"If the plate's empty, lick it," says A smiling. "But on the other hand the plates not really all that empty, is it? Some dregs waiting further disposal, I suppose, but now's the time to move on to another segment of this rather unresolved text. Isn't it?"

"O.k. It just so happens I can give the opening effort toward another part of the manuscript. Maybe a more straightforward segment . . . maybe."

III: A, B, C, Kiet Hoang, Waldo Jelliffe

ON BATAM ISLAND, KIET Hoang seldom dreamed, mostly because he seldom slept. For as long as he could remember whenever the soft relaxation that signaled the start of slumber settled in, he saw the same scene in his mind. He stood in the sagging doorway of his family's house outside of Phnom Penh watching , about 100 yards away on the almost uniform furrows of the family garden, his father writhing and spitting blood, until one of the teenagers in khaki shorts emptied the rounds left in his AK-47 into the bouncing body. That dispatch apparently gave sanction to the next step, the frenzied machetto-ing of Kiet's mother and little sister, who had been forced to watch the execution of his father.

Kiet re-enacted each night, as sleep threatened, the sharp intake his breath took at the scene, the lift his stomach seemed to detach from whatever held it in place and stream upward as if he had jumped off a thousand foot cliff into an enveloping blackness that throttled him in the plunge. The possibility of rest only triggered a convincing expulsion of all his innards belching upwards to burst their way out through his eyes, ears, nostrils in a sigh that he believed doubled him over, even as he remained prone on the thin mattress of the barracks.

On poorer nights the enveloping blackness and the detached stomach feeling culminated in actual nausea and he'd retch into the porcelain low bowl he kept beneath his bed. It was the shower of his sister's limbs as she tried to fend off the blades that pinwheeled in his mind. He worried that he hadn't tried to intervene, the distance was too far, yet some gesture he thought should have been made. But he had calculated and calculated and turned away, weaving his way back toward the kitchen area of the house–screams filling his head. First striding then running out the back of the house into the bamboo thicket some forty feet beyond the back doorway. Through the thicket until he reached a large live-oak tree, half dead, that in its huge trunk had a hollowed out place where he had spent the safest, softest, best moments of his twelve years. He stayed there that night and through the next day, hearing screams from adjacent farms, and his sister's torment interiorly until his vomit supplanted the remembered, agonized whine.

And it was in the dense, almost chill of the tree that he collected himself and heard another interior voice–an insistent but quiet, declarative voice that said, slowly, distinctly—"you must be very careful now, very cautious, very deliberate. They mean to kill you. And you have nothing to protect you, but your caution and your careful planning, and your willingness to hide, to deceive, and to keep moving, constantly ahead of them, in front of them, beyond them. But carefully, thoughtfully, never impulsively." The voice summoned him from the future, he was sure of it. The voice was decades older than he was, wiser, far more determined. He need only listen carefully to the voice. If he listened and followed, he would be saved. He knew it.

And the voice told him to rest till after midnight on the second day and then start out due north and west. And to travel only until sunrise. Find water. Rest in the fields, covered up from the sunlight, eat what berries he could find after dusk, and then again after midnight set out toward the north and west, toward the Thai border.

Some nights he heard only the mosquito whine as a single long running note, at the very pitch of his sister's screaming. The earth seemed endlessly moist, spongy, the bushes so thick that it was easier to crawl than push branches and reeds aside. On the second night he crawled a while and then turned over and lay quietly, imagining that if he should die, it would not be so difficult or unpleasant. He thought of his mother and sister being slowly hacked up and he cried believing shortly he would join them, but his death would be soft and deliberate and without screaming. Just as he imagined saying yes to death, the voice began speaking again, dismissing his surrender, telling him to turn over and get another mile or two in before sunrise.

It interested him how implacable the voice was–sounding a bit like his father or his uncle, as if eyeing him thoughtfully and then sipping some tea. "You may be discouraged now. That is normal, predictable, but of no importance. The task is always simpler than the thought about the task. One elbow in front of another, one pull forward, then another. It's quite simple. Rest in the daylight. In another day or two the hunger will subside. Look only for water. Concentrate on getting water, and the rest will flow to you."

In the day's heat it seemed his mother was tending to things around him; he rested in gauzy semi-consciousness and imagined she was singing beside him, doing the chores he wished he now could do, not the endless night crawling. He would survive.

Maybe it was that success that kept him up at night, walking among the barracks workers.

As if the reeds of their breathing required him to crouch and slither through them, all the while making sure they were okay, needing nothing, and safe. And safe, humming sleep through the night like mosquitos. Once in a while he imagined he might indeed crawl on the barracks floor, work his way under their beds, across the splintered boards to the shower area, and then back into his own room. And if they awoke and watched him, would they report him to the supervisor–this strange barracks captain who crawled among them at night?

Blood and flesh chips awaited his dreaming, his sister's screaming matched his own interior calculating voice, supremely calculating and choosing always to survive. What were her eight year old arms against flailing machetes? Between her screams he heard, again and again the hissing, clicking sound of the blades doing so quickly their detaching work. Would a cry from him have given them pause, summoned them into realization of what they were actually doing? Or at the least she would have known that her dismemberment meant something to him, meant something to her beyond the stark, dumb inevitability of entirely natural happening. First the father, then the mother, then the daughter, then cleaning the blades. He worried that they used his own sprinkling can to clean the blades. What other uses would they find for his boyish implements? And the hemorrhaging bodies left in the garden, blackening the soil. Left to blacken the soil.

Some nights he imagined wakening the Filipino workers and asking them, was there only one end in life: to blacken the soil? And wouldn't that be the perfect trade-off–you blackened the soil and in return the screaming stopped, the fevered whine softly spun down into a murmuring insect sound in the thicket, a sound that kept you crawling in the darkness toward the Thai border.

But on the fourteenth day he reached Vietnam. What he imagined was north and west turned out to be south and east. Crawling had become natural for him, relieving, comforting.

He grew dizzy standing up. He had found water along the way but not much else. Some berries, bitter and acrid, contributing to his dysentery. And then on the morning of the fourteenth day as he was remembering his home's doorway and the slumping image of his struggling father, the voice said firmly, "This day you must move in the daylight. It will be all right, simply stand and walk toward your destiny." And he repeated the phrase to himself as he stood and walked, "I am walking toward my destiny." At noon he could not walk any further and he slumped forward, dumped by the side of the dusty narrow highway where a cart stopped long enough to get him thrown into the bags of rice beneath a thick burlap, hiding them both from the sweet, soft sunlight.

When the burlap was pulled back, it was night time and a very thin, very short woman stood peering over the cart edge and tapping herself on her chest and saying softly something that sounded like "mi Jen-ah." She kept repeating the phrase and tapping her chest, "Mi Jen-ah" speaking the syllables distinctly, as if to force comprehension on him. She smiled at him, offered him a drink from a wooden bowl; it was the clearest coldest best water he had ever tasted in his life. She kept up the repetition, verging now on chant: "Jen–nah, Jen-nah."

He finally caught on he was to repeat the phrase, and when he did the woman's face took on a delight that seemed to him glowed more than the hanging lantern beyond the cart. Her epic smile seemed to banish the darkness and float of soft sheet of whiteness over his fears. She held up a second bowl and he quickly scooped all the warm rice out of it, racing toward his cracked lips. But she hooked his arm with the first bowl and tugged on it, preventing him from eating. "Slow," she said somewhat harshly. He wondered if she would deny him the food, but gradually she let him pull his hand to his mouth. "Slow," she repeated. "Slow," in a language he had never heard. She seemed intent on not letting him eat the whole scoop of rice. And he at least understood that restraint enough to comply.

Such compliance generated an even broader smile–so that was what "slow" meant. Two expressions to be treasured: "Jen-ah, . . . and slow."

When sleep seemed hardest and Kiet sat on his cot in the barracks wondering how so many could slumber their way past the past, he replayed in his mind the sounds of the woman Jen-ah talking to a man. The sounds he heard then, only began to make sense as his grasp of English now thickened in the decades since he heard that conversation. He now knew he had heard the phrase, over and over again: "he's only twelve" to which the man countered something like, "my point, my point exactly. We can't be responsible for him. They'll know he's not ours. They'll know." Each time the man spoke the woman grew silent. And he heard her crying, as if the man's words pointed to something terrible. As if his words blurred into the hacking spray of his sister's machetto-ed limbs.

And in the evening of third day with the woman and the ar-guing man, two girls Kiet's age came and led him away telling him in broken phrases in his own language they would soon be on a boat and heading toward safety. He did not see Jenna and the man again, but the woman blended into his memories of his mother so that sometimes he had to set the two memories apart by physically placing each woman in a separate part of the barracks. Doubtless that also convinced the other workers that indeed their boss was suffering from some strange illness that made him all the more dangerous and unpredictable.

The two girls were perhaps only a year older than he was, but they were infinitely superior to him in getting food, shelter, rest along the way to the vaunted boat of safety. And for reasons he later tried to fathom, they took great interest in protecting him.

He had never gotten along with his younger sister and now to be so dependent on these girls was an almost disturbing reversal.

But just as they predicted once they reached the coast in a mangrove cove there was the escape boat, a 50-foot craft with two outboard motors on the back end and a tent tossed mid-ship big enough to hold perhaps thirty people. At one end of the tent there was a pail with a fire in it, and on a grill above the fire a large clay tureen tossing steam into the evening sky. Beyond the tureen on the front deck were large wooden barrels, apparently holding fuel. The girls led him to the tureen and ladled out some soup in a bamboo bowl for him. And he was sipping the too hot liquid, the engines started and the boat moved away from the mangrove. Some of the soup spilled in the sudden lurch forward. Soon enough the girls moved him to the center of the tent area and put down a towel for all three to lie on. And with the hot soup flooding into him he began to fall asleep to the whacking whine of swung machetes. There was something counteringly magical about the rocking motion of the boat as it crested the small waves of the sea out from the coast, and a rhythm to the little pound the hull made over each crest, the little lunge forward toward the wider ocean, as if deliberately draining away memory.

And there was the assurance of thirty others slumped on the deck and sleeping. Kiet knew that sleep would forever be deepest if he could hear adjacent breathing. Crowds purged memory. And perhaps for the very first time since his escape he bridged across terror and remorse into something so delicious and trustworthy, an envelope of absolution that seemed to dissolve him into the towel, into the sleeping girls beside him, into the thirty refugees chugging their way out into the ocean of imagined opportunity.

Gunfire destroyed all that. Gunfire lit up the tent. Gunfire ignited the barrel closest to the soup, spreading orange light undulating through the tent so that faces astonished and afraid appeared like disks in the smokey darkness to Kiet. The girls were screaming, and in the pandemonium it became clear that another boat had pulled alongside and angry, well-armed intruders had come aboard. And when anyone stood up sputtering gunfire put them down again. So they hugged the deck and Kiet understood the crying came naturally enough from memory of his sister's splintering arms. For a while he thought all he had to do to end everything was simply stand up, gesture toward retribution and be snuffed out. For a while he imagined his mother was motioning to him, bidding him to stand up. His sister gestured to him called him forward, beckoned him to stand up. But the oil smell of the deck and the cool moisture pressing on his cheek, and the racket of sobbing kept him flattened. He felt an arm cross his back, cross his back fully and tuck under his ribs. He swiveled to watch the older girl pull him closer, either as protection for herself, or to stifle his evident urge to get up. He smiled at her and she closed her eyes as someone, malevolent and powerful crouched beside them. A gun barrel pried her arm off of him, and suddenly she was yanked upward and then slapped twice so that blood flowed out of her nose. Kiet hugged the deck tighter. She was hauled further away back aft toward the small cabin on the boat, away from most of the sprawled passengers. Someone stood up. Gunfire put them down, a burst of slugs shearing off an arm, so that blood rain fell on Kiet's back. And then he saw that whoever had taken the girl away was now pinioning her against the cabin and stripping her clothes off.

The stripper clamped her against the lone wooden structure on the boat and dropped off his shorts. She started screaming, but his elbow pressed in harder smothering the scream into a furtive gurgling sound. Kiet stared at her turned, slammed face, and he felt a sudden inner compulsion to jump up and save her or die trying, but once again a calculating voice took over his mind; whatever was going on would be over soon enough and getting upright would only bring bullets. But immediately the other sister voided his calculations. She lunged upward toward the fellow's back, unleashing a banshee scream that seemed to overwhelm the others with rifles, stun them into mute witness. Her hawk-like detonations filled the tent area and she grappled onto the fellow's back, pulling at his hair, nails raking across his eyes as if to pluck them out. And her energy pulled Kiet into the fray too. He lunged against the fellows legs, biting at the backs of his naked knees and howling like a wounded dog. The fellow swiveled around, tossing the girl from him, and punched Kiet's back, while kicking free of Kiet's lock around his legs. Suddenly others were pulling Kiet away and pummeling him with rifle butts.

He felt has ribs crack and soon enough the butt of an older rifle snapped his jaw across consciousness.

When he woke he was aware of bobbing in the sea, felt himself bound to the two girls although one was unconscious, bound tightly so that he could feel their breathing, join their sighing and sobbing as the barrel that contained the three of them slipped further and further away from the exiting boat. He felt a certain warm wetness down his legs and realized it must be blood from the youngest girl. He worried that the blood might fill the barrel and sink it. The warmth flowed over and into his sneakers and it seemed there was a bit of play in the ropes around their ankles, but any movement only sent the barrel bobbing over toward the side. Eventually the conscious girl threw up and she began making a sigh that seemed to call out to someone, anyone, for rescue. He suggested she stop hollering. There was no point. The boat was long gone and the evening sky darkened overhead. Kiet swiveled to see if he could release some of the bindings around their waists and shoulders, necks, but the ropes were too tight. He sensed soon enough the fibers would cut their skins and meanwhile the bobbing, bobbing of the barrel induced nausea. The eyes of the bleeding girls rolled upward just as the moon's paring came over the lip of the barrel. The other girl's screaming turned slowly to muted sobs and hysterical hand flapping beneath their locked elbows. The blood warmth over his feet turned soggy and cold and he realized that death was certain, as certain as the rocking motion churning his innards. Doubtless it would be better to tilt the barrel over and fill with sea water and surrender to sure, sloshing doom. And if not doom, then at least to delicious sleep, fed as much by fatigue as terror.

Once again in the barracks the voice repeated softly, insistently, "But this sleep is only for renewal. It is not the end, not surrender, not doom. It is the rest before the effort–storage before the surge." Gathering torque before the supreme test, which Kiet perfectly understood in his sagging slumber he would pass, indeed triumph over leading to ultimate riches and erasure of his sister's splittered limbs.

When he awoke in seawater he noticed that the barrel was not rocking, not turning, not moving. On its side now, his view if he lifted his head (which felt too heavy to lift) revealed only beach sand. The younger girl bound so tightly to him continued to breathe, with a soft mindless sigh at the end of each breath. The other bound girl was clearly dead and spoiling, her skin under the clamped rope gushing pus and peeling. At first he imagined he was dreaming. Could they actually be out of the sea?

-§-

At Serena B starts, characteristically, with an objection. "I understand the early traumas—a bit overloaded, but understandable. Okay I see where he comes from, his horrible experiences. All terrific stuff. I couldn't survived it, but I don't get how he gets from rolling up on the beach in a barrel of dead girls to working a kitchen in the Sheraton in KL and from there to Batam Island. Are you going to lay all that out, or are we just supposed to accept it. In which case I don't accept it."

"Serendipity underlays all of life," A says smiling. "And American lawyers are everywhere looking for quick remuneration, isn't that so?"

"Unlike British barristers, I suppose," B says.

"It happens as I tell it to you," C says with some impatience. "I'm not sure how he winds up in the Sheraton in KL. How does anyone end up working in a Sheraton, especially if you're young and stateless? But I know precisely how he gets from there to Batam Island. It's his language skill. How many itinerant salad sou-chefs in Southeast Asia speak both Cambodian and English, with a good grasp of Vietnamese salad-speak and some Filipino to boot."

"Which Filipino?" A asks, proud it seems of his own language expertise.

"Which dialect?" C asks.

"Yes, which dialect? Tagalog, or something else."

"Let's say something else, something from the southern Philippines. Something semi Arabic, okay?"

"Not okay," B says, "the whole drift seems bogus, and worse than bogus, boring. Very boring."

"I'd like to hear about the lawyers and the language expertise," A says, smiling again.

"Well I haven't written it all out, but eventually I'll show that you're right, serendipity does play a role. Three American lawyers object to the structure of a beet salad, ordered at the would-be Tiki-Hut manqué in KL's tallest, most glass filled Sheraton. Maybe too much or maybe not enough Feta (incidentally rather hard to get in Malaysia). And they demand to see the salad chef, who it turns out does not speak English, but sheepishly puts forth young Kiet, who Jenna-trained speaks perfect Presbyterian Woman Missionary English."

B interrupts, "Glass-filled is the right phrase. I stayed there once and by God each corner room all the way up had a shower room with transparent glass overlooking the damn cricket pitch some 56 flights down. You could splash naked confident anyone looking up with binoculars could see your privates."

"Irrelevant dicta," A asserts. "I want to hear what the lawyers said and how Kiet gets to Batam Island."

C continues, "In their objecting conversation it somehow comes out that Kiet speaks Cambodian, and a little Vietnamese and some Filipino—I don't know which dialect or whatever, maybe tribal language if you'd prefer. But the key point it is he's at least trilingual and that's a solution to big labor problems in Batam."

"American lawyers worried about Batam labor relations?" B asks.

"Of course. Of course labor relations, but only in so far as those restrict cash flow to those lawyer's private clubs in the states. The smooth creation of Velcro strips is not happening, cash is not being generated because the superintendents can't communicate with their exploited workers. And here, suddenly over a mangled beet salad, comes salvation—young energetic, well spoken, full of subservient English—awash in 'God willings'"

"What?" B asks.

"Kiet keeps Jenna's training always at the forefront of any assertion, 'God willing'. Let's say it bedevils the lawyers, who incidentally have lost their shirts in abortive shrimp farms and see dollars firmly velcroed to their shining asses." C explains.

"Jesus!" B says.

"So the lawyers quickly designate the youngest of them to take Kiet to Batam and make him top manager of the immigrant recruits scraped up with the irresistible spatula of payment in U.S. dollars. It turns out Presbyterian missionary and corporate leadership speak the same language. The gelatin of soft coercion firms up in Batam, and the rectification of shrimp disaster appears possible. Good enough?"

"So what do you have for us?" A asks.

"Is it going to be gory?" B asks

"Eventually it will, but certainly not now," C answers. "For now it's a story of Waldo and Kiet finding a peculiar common ground, our kind of common ground."

"And what does that mean?" B says brusquely. "Some of claptrap about getting old mutually and looking deathly together?"

"Why not?"

"It's boring. I'd rather have gore."

"You'll get plenty at the end, but for now I'm telling you about nascent brotherhood."

"Cross cultural fraternity," A says, "I love it. It's so American. Ismael/Queequeg; Huck/Jim; Mel and Danny. I love it."

"You won't eventually," C says, "But for now, just listen."

The Riches of This World, Part C

(Waldo and his Kiet)

There was a point where Waldo Jelliffe looked forward to long plane flights. The oversize seat he paid for, the tidy white napkins rimming his individually selected meals, the kindly thick smiles of ever solicitous flight attendants, seemed a balm made for transport out of the ignorant and ignored skeptical realm of the news room. Plane drone seemed a better place to be. Did the noise silence his fears of full acceptance? He wondered occasionally if airborne unbalance banished or overcame somehow self-doubt. They might mock him in the city room, but he got to cruise away at 35,000 feet with ever widening solicitation all around him, in a seat that truly pushed back into apparently receptive space. Receptive space. He wondered if that did not underlie his delight in long monologues before LP in the dark stained wood of lodge house on Batam Island. The smiling Cambodian always met him in neat shorts and wonderfully de-mudded sandals and led him limply to the company Toyota President sedan.

Waldo had learned that free cocktails on international flights carried a severe penalty. He stuck to seltzer water, ginger ale, and in the last hours to Mr. and Mrs. T bloody Mary mix in a can, a kind of salty liberation libation. He just felt he was in control of his life when cruising toward Batam, in the plane, in the Toyota President model, in the cypress slatted lodge, and before him LP in khaki shorts and spiffed-up sandals. Everything fell into place. The cabbage palms studding the barracks marched to his directives, as did the soft warm air.

"LP I feel so much better here. Maybe purged of New England strictures and general preachiness. Maybe that's it."

"Yes," LP replied, ever attentive if not entirely comprehending what Waldo was signaling.

"I come here to rejuvenate. Do you know that term, 'rejuvenate,' a terrific word and so true, 'Rejuvenat-tatzione'" Waldo said wallowing in delight at his ability to Italianate a phrase to emphasize its aptness, its unalloyed joy of expression. "Rejuvenat-tatzione! Try it, LP, let it rip forth!"

LP nodded but silently stared at his ridged toenails.

"So let's have some B & B. I brought the old replenishment bottle, so there's plenty. Get the glasses and whatever's left in the cupboard." And Waldo flopped down on the rattan couch, threw his arms over the tired back cushions and relaxed back, eyes trained on the overhead beams. "Be quick, LP, be quick. For I am sore afraid, filled with fear and trembling, since none of the pillars I live by are here present, thank God! None of the rules here apply. None of the responsibilities. You fly out here and land utterly free, unjudged, liberated by your irrelevancy, although in truth I know about that at home more than I wish to accept, or even acknowledge. You probably don't feel irrelevant, do you LP? Go ahead pour the drinks. I don't need ice, nor would I get it here, or bacon for that matter. Of course you're not irrelevant, are you? How could you be? You make everything happen. You are the essential conduit. Do you know that term, 'conduit'? It's what you are. When the bosses need to tell the workers what to do and when, why you're the only one who can pass the message along. More than pass it along. Get it accomplished. I'm not much of a conduit. Not a good listener, Suzan says. Ah, yes, she says it often, even when she's not medicated. Medicated—another good term. Do you know it?"

"Med eh kay ted," LP echoed.

"Very good. You're a terrific mimic. First rate. Have your drink and I'll try to listen to you, with, with *empathy*. That's what I need, Suzan says, empathy! The world needs empathy, and doesn't have it. Suzan's right even if medicated. She's right. It's the essential term, isn't it? The Japanese got it right, didn't they? *Enryo*—their term for it. Holding back. Staunching their own convictions and giving others room to breathe, really to act in ways that made sense to them. Not imposing your position, your attitude on anyone. But listening, really listening so as to hear what truly was being said. I know you're good at it. Everyone in the front office says so. You listen. You really listen, and they," Waldo waved at the barracks beyond the shivering cabbage palms, "they know you hear them. So they listen to you. The front office knows how important you are to making sure everyone works and is happy. Everyone! God, you make everyone so productive. Another wonderful word. The front office loves hearing that you're so '**productive**'. And productive means profitable, the more Velcro latches, the more dollars pour in. Productive is Profit."

Having made that proclamation Waldo pressed harder on the back of the couch; he pulled a print pillow out from behind him and flipped it onto the thick gold carpet surrounding the couch. "It's so much easier being a Jelliffe on Batam, LP, can you imagine it? I don't suppose you can. What is lineage out here? What is family fortune in the barracks? Among the peons? I bet you don't get that word, **peons**, do you? Maybe nobody should know the word. Maybe, maybe not. What do you think?"

LP didn't answer, just drank in one rushed motion the brandy Waldo had poured.

"What does being a Jelliffe mean out here? Everybody out here could be swept away by God's giant hand. Right? In fact you were just recently, flushed away, tsunami-ed away, weren't you? No heritage. No memory of forebearers who started your country, wrote your sacred documents, suffered your revolutionary war. Right? Freed of all that crap? Ready to be swept away, washed away, over flooded while rushing for higher land. Lighting out for the territory as the monster sea closes in. Right? Jeliffism sucks, isn't it so? Isn't it?"

Waldo poured two more drinks, and leaned even further forward to watch a large Palmetto bug scurry across the wide floor boards toward the front screenless porch. For a moment he imagined the bug had been seduced by the swaying 40 watt lantern hanging over the outside railing. There was suddenly a mewing in darkness beyond the lantern, as if an assembly of chorusing mosquitoes was bidding the Palmetto bug on.

"I'm going to show you what Jelliffe heritage is someday," Waldo continued after a long swallow of his brandy. "I'm going to show you and you'll know it, yes, know it from the inside. I'm going to take you back with me."

LP said, "Know it. Know it."

"Yeah, know it from the inside. Jelliffe heritage . . . can you spread it on toast? Can you?"

"Know it." LP repeated. "Know it."

"Will it cure anything? No nothing. Least of all, a sick wife. Someday you'll come back with me and I'll show you Jelliffe heritage." Waldo poured another drink and shook his head slowly. "Of course there's that issue of a visa, always a visa, my stateless friend. So I won't bring you back for a while. It will take care and attention to get you back to Worcester. Just don't lose heart."

"Lose heart," LP repeated, as if savoring the sentiment.

-§-

B interrupted the reading, "I don't see where this is going. Why are you telling us about Waldo and LP/Kiet? I assume Kiet is LP, is that not so? I can barely remember Waldo."

"Of course," C answered. "Waldo was Lewis's editor/mentor. And I'm setting it up so that eventually LP kills Waldo."

"Wow! What kind of spoiler alert are you tossing us now?"

"Okay, maybe it won't turn out that way."

"Jesus! Sleaze ball tactics of floating dread eventualities, and then shouting, 'Made you look. Made you look!' Let's grow up and work on real literature. Real story-telling. And who could buy all that crap about Jelliffe heritage?"

C answers, "Since we don't have any here, can't have any here, it's not surprising you assume felt-heritage has to be crap."

A says, "It's true enough. We're not going to point to any pre-decessors, are we? No predecessors, and no followers on. Just a big one generation whose children are in some kind of exile, since they can't really stay here. Of course you'd be feeling nostalgic for some some solidity, in the old country that was not in fact old for you."

B says, "Everything is old for you. You relish antiquity. It's endemic among Brits. I see that. But I don't care about it. The point is it's getting to be boring. Why follow it?"

"Heritage is a path out of boredom," A says.

"Let's go back to Kiet/LP killing Waldo. I'm sorry your children and mine can't continue living here, so they have to live somewhere, like all of us—somewhere near death, somewhere on the abyss, elsewhere. Elsewhere. The Grand Elsewhere. Come on Kiet, kill Waldo."

The Riches of This World, Part D

(Waldo's Fate, a Play in Two Scenes)

The curtain opens on the strangely empty psych ward of Worcester City Hospital. A polished green linoleum floor shows the wide swaths of floor buffer semi-circles in the dusty overhead fluorescent light. Suzan Jelliffe stands center stage in a white dressing gown, like a marble statue almost a perfect inert rendering save for her right leg quivering every other minute for a few seconds, causing her to tap her bare feet. Waldo in a grey pin-striped suit stands two feet from her, extending (what he hopes is perceived as tenderly) his right hand toward her hip. She ignores the gesture and says:

Suzan: You come dressed like the outside world, and I'm not sure how I feel about that. Sometimes jealous, I guess, since you smell of freedom and deliverance and choice—mostly choice. And I don't get those. I don't. And I know it's not right to be so pathetic, but there it is, isn't it? Have you brought news?

Waldo: Hardly. The world remains as unattractive as always.

Suzan: You can say that. I can't.

I do: It's my prerogative and curse.

Suzan: You're so burdened. It's much lighter here. See. I'm floating. Float with me. Or better yet take me away.

Waldo: You can leave at any time. Just speak the word, my love.

Suzan: So I'm self-bound, is that it? Then unbind me. Oh I know — not your task. But your suit seems half funereal. Are you going to one?

Waldo: Only the one of your conviction. Why don't we just leave this place, or maybe go to a better one in Connecticut? I'm dressed for your exit. I really don't see how you get better here.

Suzan: The state says I'm a danger to myself, since I took all those zantacs and lost even a gag reflex. Lost even a gag reflex. Can you believe those were the words I heard when I came back? The very first words. 'We couldn't even get a gag reflex when you came in.' An enviable achievement, apparently. Something they hadn't seen—not even a gag reflex. Something beyond the greatest Jelliffe achievement. Precisely beyond all lineage, all heritage, all merit, all inherited joy—not even a gag reflex.

Waldo: The state misunderstood your motives. I made that clear to them. Curing an upset stomach, lessening stress, is not self-destructive.

Suzan: One hundred and twenty Zantacs lessens a lot of stress, placates a surging stomach, don't you think? Or is it an invitation to something other, and so it was. So it was. I told them, told you, will tell you, about the great warm feeling I had floating away, losing that horrid gag reflex was a liberation as thrilling as,

... as ... What would say? As finding God in the sweet swirling sediment of loss. There you were in grey pin-stripes and beckoning, holding your arms up. And I know how hard that is for you. Or any physical labor. You're about as handy as a cat, an old cat and incontinent. Incontinent ... This place is a shrine to incontinence. Float away with me. We can leave the smell below, the sweet sediment of loss. Don't you see what we lost? Don't you feel it? It's as if we're at the airport and for the last time, and you help me up the ancient rattling steel pull down steps. Slowly one step at a time you walk me up the crusted rubber treads, and I get to sit in one of the wider, immediate first class seats and you kiss my neck and then you back away rather quickly it seems, and you're framed momentarily in plane archway exit at the top of the dirty steps and I call out to you and you answer in that ironic quizzical way you use to avoid all commitment, 'Yes?' And I say ever so sweetly, 'I love you.' And then poof goes the gag reflex. Come float with me.

Waldo: You're ready. We really ought to leave. Let's leave.

Suzan: Am I ready? Ready for you, you old incontinent cat? Ready to resume our incontinent life? Have I truly recovered a gag reflex? Or might it be impossible for me to imagine swallowing the emptiness you represent?

Waldo: Emptiness?

Suzan: That feeling I get every afternoon around 4, and you go off to the club and I remember to join you for dinner but instead go to bed. And in a while another day begins. I'll leave when I know for sure that you're entirely gone.

Waldo: If I believed you, I would be gone.

Suzan: So believe me. I'm not the ornament of your emptiness, the elaborate walnut carving of your Jelliffe mantel. Unless you want to float away with me.

Waldo: Actually I don't float. I'm stuck here on the ground, resting on God's footstool, afraid to peer over the edge.

Suzan: Stultified, leaving me in the vapors above. And I like it. I get to make things here, wallets, key chains, maybe gloves in the advanced classes. Maybe, yes maybe, in the advanced classes.

Waldo: Listen, let's not get stuck in this silly game of pretending we're talking about repairing whatever it is that brought you here. Discussing abstractions so that we don't have to take a step toward the smelly business of enduring each day together. We mustn't mock ourselves in this tepid silliness any longer. We only have to go home.

Suzan: But home for you is some place your tired imagination summoned long, long ago. It's a place I'm left out of—maybe worse, simply erased from. You're in the Jelliffe pew, nestled among previous Jelliffes and virtually hugging each other, while I sit alone in the choir loft. So float away with me. Away with me, outside of skittering history. I don't want to go to your home. I was only a projection there. Here I'm a free floater.

Waldo: Do you want to spend the rest of your days here? In here? Is this what 'here' means for you?

-§-

"Jesus, enough rummaging around for some ethical crap," B interrupts, "it's really boring and you need to get off the dime. Move the narrative forward."

A says, "Such American longing for telling all, unraveling all. I was beginning to get interested in the Jelliffe melodrama, and now we'll have to turn your promised violence I suppose."

"I'm not sure about that," C says, "In fact, I'm not sure about revealing Waldo's desperation."

"Desperation? What in God's name has he got to be desperate about?" B asks.

A answers, "The little depressing luggage of a name, a wife or life partner of dubious sanity, a childless horizon, a constant outside dismissal of his being in the world. Desperate sounds inevitable to me."

"You're great at making lists of meaningless items. Why not say everything on your silly list adds up to pure liberty, liberty and leverage. I could sell you a dozen Tiguans."

C says, "Let's set aside this problematic duo. I'll get back to them when they're clearer. When I'm clearer. In the meantime here's material that doubtless will illuminate previous encounters.

Please listen with at least sparse commitment." C looks intently at A and B.

"All right here's what you need to know before you tackle Part III. 'Archer's World.' All of what I'm telling you will unfold in the narrative that I'll write, but only after I've finished the crucial parts which I'll give to you eventually. It's not clear if I'll get to write them. For one thing writing that narrative, filling in that unfolding, will take a good bit of energy, and I'm aware I don't have much lately. Getting less energetic as the hairline recedes, the muscles slack, the cartilage breaks down and the libido evaporates."

"You overwrite a bit," B says.

"Agreed but pay attention to the following information:

His father arrives in Japan in the Taisho era of democracy and prosperity, an aspiring Presbyterian missionary enjoying a three year visa, and finding a ready audience in Niigata for the Christian Word. Originally focused on teaching English to high school girls, he finds one in particular irresistible and soon enough has permission to marry her. Her father is a Buddhist monk and Archer would eventually believe that the was the beginning of his father's transformation—from missionary into what Archer thought was a "lost Buddhist" ever wavering on the edge of mannered disinclination or despair. That nifty balancing act was nurtured, cultivated, curated, celebrated only because an unwavering enshrinement of Japanese Culture knitted up all the disparate parts. In the presence of what he knew fundamentally to be a superior civilization, a finer expression of human potential the father would over time first attempt to integrate Christian concepts only to reject them entirely by the time of the war's mid-point in 1943. It was a thoroughly ingratiating and predictable persuasion, Archer thought, since the war's destruction from that mid-point on could be seen, joyously as the working out of bad desires in a consummate suffering that explored all the peripheral edges of "unsatisfactoriness." Japan's incineration was ultimately explicable and survivable within a Buddhist explanation, and how instinctively the Japanese embraced that suffering, as well as the unarticulated acceptance of the Buddha's explication.

IV: A, B, C, Archer Hesseltine

AT SERENA IN A late January surprisingly suffused with spring A, B, and C agree to have the lamb *teishoku* luncheon. C seems anxious to get a serious focus for the meal. Lamb was serious, wasn't it?

"It will be New Zealand lamb," B says. "Probably the leftovers from some 'Viking Buffet' in Kyushu last week, and peppered within an inch of its sorry life, or curried so as to hide the smell."

"You seem to be looking forward to it," A says.

B flashes A a third finger.

"I want us to think about fathers today," C says, smiling since on that topic he imagines there is a fissure between A and B. A's father, classically British, in A's previous mentions of him, seems only a passing breeze of an experience, at once empty of recollection, no more than an ornament on a mantel in a room one seldom entered. B's memory is much more immediate and involving. When the topic last was discussed, B ended up singing hymns in what he claimed was the precise tone and rippling presence his father commanded in the church of the Savior in Wisconsin, or, more secularly, among the wicker furniture of their Maine summer home.

"I thought we'd dealt with that topic," B says sharply.

"We did," C concedes, but "I'm afraid we'll have to revisit it somehow to get through the next parts."

"Get through is surely the correct term, the truest word, the finest, clearest expression of what we're dealing with. So what do you have for us?"

"Doubtless something urgent," A says, "requiring a turn off of all the phones." He nods toward B.

"Not a chance. You'll just have to live vicariously through me."

"Doubtless with our lamb curry."

"Japanese curry, always a disappointment," A says. "I shouldn't have signed on."

"We get to hear about Archer's father." C interrupts.

"Is that the same Archer or whatever his name is in other of your immortal works?"

"Exactly. And now we get to hear about those early moments of maturation that determined the next decades of his life."

"Jesus, I can't wait. But, alas, I can, and with luck a phone call will rescue me."

C continues, "We have to go back to 1945 and chronicle two catastrophes that undo whatever stability young Archer had. A double whammy of sorts: first the unbelievable bombing campaign the U.S. carried to full fruition over Honshu, second and perhaps more significant for Archer, his father's bitter defection from Christian belief to Buddhist acceptance, which may or may not have occurred in direct response to the first catastrophe."

"Ah," B says "the old 'whiff of grapeshot effect.'"

"Astonishing! An historical reference from you, of all companions. What has come over you?" A says, smiling. "Akai Ito comes to Austerlitz?"

"Too cute. Too cute." B says, "let's just get on with it. But not the actual it, just your overview of the **it** that must be read some other time, some other day, some other millennium. And not by me, since I read only a paragraph of two each hour. I'm an accomplished administrator."

"Some things cannot be summarized," C responds.

"Oh, try. Try harder."

"No, you try. Take it home with you, and let me know when you're done. We'll talk then."

"If it leaves with me now, you ought to know it will go into a folder in my office, and then to stack on the top of a beige file cabinet for weekend reading, that invariably I forget to take home for the weekend, because I gave up weekend reading after my last promotion. I can designate readers who then file single page memo summaries of what I should have read. It's the new world, bucko. The triumph or success of superficiality. Deal with it."

79

"Take the story. Do your own summary. You'll want to talk. Eat your curry."

"Jesus," B says. "Is this the back story on the fellow who ends up translating accounts of atrocities carried out in Mongolia or Manchuria? He works for the Ambassador who dies in a plane crash or gets murdered or something in a couple of your earlier works?"

"Yes. Precisely. It's information you've been dying to find out."

"I only read the back covers. So I'm not really dying to find out. Why don't you just tell me?"

"Just skim it."

The Riches of This World, Part E

On March 1st, 1945 Reverend Dwayne Hesseltine, pastor of the Church of St. Mary, Yokohama City forty minutes below Tokyo, sat down with his family: son Archer, daughter Emma, wife Claire and proposed they should flee. Nightly American bombers plastered Tokyo with explosions that came closer and closer to the suburbs. Pastor Dwayne thought the decimations were like mole holes coming closer and closer to the tired tiled- roof thatch house St. Mary's congregation had provided its spiritual mentor.

"As I see it," the pastor said, "there are only two places untouched by American bombs; Hiroshima, and Kyoto. We should leave immediately for both of them.

"Dad, they will be targets, just because they haven't been targets," young Archer, age 17, said, missing the point.

"You'd think so, but that's the not the way Americans think. Someone is protecting them, someone in the American government is looking out for them. You've heard rumors that Vice President Truman has a relative in Hiroshima, and someone high up thinks Kyoto has only sacred shrines, nothing worth bombing. And bombing them would make the occupation that much more difficult. We should split up and go to two places. That way some part of the family will survive."

"I think we should all go together to the Noto peninsula or maybe Hokaido, or maybe Kyushu," Archer said with some urgency. We should stay together even if we die together."

"No," spoken slowly and softly as if to underscore maximum conviction, "staying together is not paramount, surviving is. If we choose properly, we can reassemble after this stupid war is over. Choosing properly is paramount. Splitting apart is the only answer to desecration." Pastor Dwayne said.

"We should stay together and pray for God to show us a pathway to survival," Claire said. "Trust that the Lord will provide. Jesus will not leave us destitute."

"Not destitute. Rich in glittering ashes." The pastor countered.

Emma who was eight, added, "I don't want to die."

"If we're alert and make the right choices, no one will die," Dwayne said. "Don't worry Emmi, don't worry."

"The right choice is for us all to stay together," Claire said, "and move toward either of the places your father has specified."

"Claire, look, the war will end soon. Japan is defeated but doesn't know that yet. Soon enough it will understand—when the B-17s and 29s close off sunshine. Soon enough," he slumped a bit at the low table, and as if to underline the end of Japan uncoiled his legs extending them under the table like some hapless *gaijin*.

"Papa," Emma chided him, a reference to the many times he'd taught to sit Japanese style on her crossed shins.

"Soon enough we'll be sitting in chairs and no longer squatting over our toilets." Dwayne half laughed. "We need to decide who's going where."

"We'll go together," Claire said quietly. "Whatever happens we'll be together. Together."

The good pastor suddenly resonated to her firm tone. The clarity of her conviction seemed freeing. He felt a certain calmness descending on the family scene, as if somehow he had floated above the fear he felt. He wondered if extending his legs had signaled a release from Japan's strictures, the clamped feeling in his numbed legs. Lately he had given up praying, preferring to imagine he would meditate, focusing only on his breath. Nothing had come either of praying or meditating save a certain sense of irony about either enterprise, a syrupy laughter at himself, more so at his pious wife's traditional graces before each meal. He recognized the distant detonations at Yokohama harbor or more nearly in Tokyo itself heralded an internal breakup of something or other that had organized his life, as he watched his adopted country spiral deeper into atrocity and madness. He imagined the Master said, Now focus on the breath, think only of its in and out slow motion and do not contemplate family extinction. But of course "do not" meant "do," upending anything like relief. Fear always came back and stronger, more present than any scheme of adjustment. None the less, he looked at Claire's quiet face and felt her strength of conviction was more than balm to his dread. Perhaps grace and realization could be linked somehow.

-§-

B looked up from his copy and asked, "Where do they end up? Which city? And more importantly, you said his wife was Japanese. What kind of Japanese woman is called Claire?"

"They opt for Kyoto, but that means they must travel to Tokyo as there is still one train and one bus line down to Kyoto that hasn't been destroyed. I'm still working on the Claire issue. You'll get clarity when I get it."

"I can't say I really care about the Claire issue, as you put it so inelegantly. So tell me about their life in unbombed Kyoto and the war's end."

"They don't make it. They never get to Kyoto. They reach Tokyo in the later afternoon of March 8th. "

"Ohhh," A says. "They reach Ueno on the 8th?"

"Yes."

"How unfortunate," A continues. "Yet Archer survives, doesn't he? Or are you rewriting things, even as we wait on our lamb curry? Incidentally, doubtless you've both noticed that the *katakana* for 'stew' literally sounds out: 'shit too.'"

"Ah," B says, "such a fucking vulgarian! I take it something horrible happens in Tokyo on the 8th?"

"More like the 9th and 10th," A answers. "the infamous fire-bombing raids. Lemay's legions literally ignited the oxygen in the air of Tokyo, incinerating everything. Everything. Every living and every inert thing."

"Shit too!" B said. "A little American shit-too as payback for Pearl Harbor ... "

C interrupts this turn in the conversation, striking, surprisingly a solemn, serious tone. "You need to read the crucial part. What Archer and his father discuss that night of the 8th explains everything, determines everything in the next decade of Archer's life."

"Can't you just summarize what you're getting at? Invariably your explanations save me time and energy."

"I cannot."

"Oh, sweet Jesus. But only after our curry, which I see now is arriving. I'll tackle your slow prose in the cab back to the dealership."

"It's not long, just a few pages, while the curry cools," C said. "Put yourself out, for a change."

The Riches of This World, Part F

Archer's question: "If you want to escape the maelstrom, why go deeper into it?" provided a quarrelsome track on which his family rode directly into Tokyo on March 8th 1945. Archer understood that the one bus/train line left to Kyoto began in Tokyo, but he was convinced walking directly overland was preferable, certainly safer. The bombing of Tokyo had been relentless—how could going anywhere near the place be safe? If Kyoto was sanctuary there had to be some safer route to get there. It seemed to Archer his father was seeking immolation somehow, a point he discussed with his mother whose only response was a soft, "God willing." Emma had been struck dumb with terror ever since the first bomb fell near them in Yokohama. She listened to the discussion of fleeing with a stunned sadness and deeply swaddled hysteria.

His father woke Archer after midnight on the 8th and took him upstairs to the sacristy. "I wanted you to know these things over time and I had rehearsed how to say them to you in the course of weeks, hopefully months, but all that vaporized in this," he gestured toward the thunderclaps outside. I wanted to tell you that I've come to recognize Japan's strengths, its absolute wisdom and the utter bankruptcy of western Christianity. I wanted to let you track my evolution to the acceptance that there is no god, no Jesus, no resurrection, no salvation, but only a process of getting beyond any of those furrows that may have led fruitfully to some weird garden somewhere, but not the world itself. Not reality as we live it each day. I wanted you to walk that path with me so that together we could experience the relief of getting beyond our desires for coherence and progress, beyond the very stupidity of hoping for anything. But that cannot happen now. Because this threatens every thought, every aspiration. In this, our truly lived experience, there is nothing to allow us the time needed to get through these perceptions."

Archer still groggy from being dragged into consciousness and hauled upstairs for enlightenment, said, "Perceptions?"

"Yes. Yes, things you take for granted without thinking about them. Articles of faith that I cannot subscribe to. Do you understand that? There's no time to argue, only to listen. Do you hear?"

"Hear what?"

"The clicking of your brain's connectors. Go ahead trash what remains of sleep, but listen to me Arch, listen carefully. There is no god, no Christ, no salvation. There is only the steady slosh of everything and nothing."

"Everything and nothing?"

"Yes. Yes! I've come to understand the insignificance of self. Undoubtedly Japan taught me that. We just sit in the slosh and move with it in the directions it takes of its own, forward or back, upward or downward. Inward or outward, or inert or raging. It makes no difference. All that matters (including mattering itself) is how those beyond us relapse into the slosh, how we accept its motion. The slosh is supremely indifferent to our aspirations or our bleatings. We dwell in its acceptance of itself. Nothing more."

"No right or wrong?"

"Only the slosh, the process. That's the liberation. The last dreg of Jesus, his ethics, counts for nothing because nothing counts in the slosh. That's what I had hoped to lead you to, but there's no time now. Just accept what I tell you. No god, no Jesus, no faith, no hope."

"Dad, how can you keep going forward?"

"That's the trick, the ultimate deliverance: you recognize that 'going forward' is the real enemy, actually the real impossibility. Stop 'wanting to go forward' and everything clarifies in its pointlessness. You cannot suffer if you cannot hope. I can tell you that, but it takes study and focus to get there on your own, so I betray myself by speaking. But what can I do? I wanted to walk with you toward this deliverance, but there's no chance. And I realizing wanting that chance betrayed its possibility."

"What do you want from me?"

"Just listen. I will tell you and eventually you'll see what you'll do where you'll go."

Archer listened more carefully, aware now instructions somehow would be involved. Light from the myriad offering candles stuck in their metal holders lining the side railings cast a weak orange glow to the sacristy. Archer imagined there would be a myriad candle lighters passing through the church as detonations decorated the life beyond the church and shudders of the building unbalanced even the lighting of one candle to another. Prayer was strongest Archer guessed in the face of imminent destruction. But the church of the Redeemer was starkly empty now. Of all buildings in south Tokyo perhaps the church alone had a basement—testament, Archer wondered, to the likelihood and expectation of explosion. There was only the sullen acknowledgement among Japanese Christians (ever dwindling in number and attentiveness) to their vulnerability apart from catacombs of survival beneath the earth's dirty hide. Come and hide with us below. You'll be safe there, until this nutcase father shouts that safety is mirage and nothing you believe has any viability. Is he crazy, Archer wondered, turning over his idea that this father had taken Christian belief to its final resting place at the foot of Mt. Fuji. What had been revealed? Stress driven him nuts? For the very first time, and eventually he knew, the only time it suddenly occurred to Archer that the Dad of his models, the Dad of his protectors was in fact deranged, damaged goods, unfit to assume the role he had been cast in. How could that be? How could an assignment be so misplaced, dislodged and tainted?

"I can see you're pulling back. Don't. Just listen to me. When the time comes head north. You're right about that. Head north into the hills. Get far away. Find safety. Find it. Don't pray. It's useless. Stay in the slosh. Process is indifferent to anything that happens to us. Give up striving. No Jesus, no faith, no hope. Watch them as they cope, learn from them. Study them. They cope automatically, involuntarily and it's settling, soothing, freeing. No Jesus, no faith, no hope. Get beyond all that. Relax beyond that. Get dressed. I want you to set out now. Listen to me. Get dressed and go north into the hills, toward safety, but don't seek it. Simply flow into it. Focus on your breathing. Concentrate only on that in-and-out motion, let the slosh do the rest. There's absolute safety there."

"I don't want safety."

"Stop wanting. Set out. Do as I tell you. Now."

"I can't leave you here. I can't leave Emma. I just can't."

"They're going to die. Here. I'm going to die here. Death is here. You can't die here. I won't allow it."

"You won't allow it? What are you thinking? Are you in control of death?"

"Even in the slosh, I am. I am."

-§-

At Serena, B looked up from the manuscript. "My curry's getting cold," he said smiling. "And maybe your story is getting a bit hot. Are you referencing here a little mass *seppuku?* Really?"

"People did that all over Tokyo, when the conflagration boiled over. Lemay's fire ignited the air itself," C said. "The air burned. All you could do, the only control you had was choosing death. Volition. Agency. Death. The choice allowed. That allowance only. Three inches of freedom—a three inch space of choice. What her foot against the door permitted you. All that death allowed."

"Death's little treat, then, your volition to die, and the others with you. Pity there wasn't a *kyukuo* to jump in front of. How did the good reverend do it? Knife in the stomach? Bullet to the head? Just swell screaming into the flames?" B said.

A said, "The latter if you care to read it all the way through."

"I've caught the drift," B said, spooning some of the curry into his lips. "So hellfire reaches the good but disillusioned pastor and his family."

"Except for Archer," C said.

"So he did light out for the territory," B said.

"Yes, indeed," A answered. "He headed north into the hills."

"How did Daddy persuade him?" B asked.

"No persuasion. Orders. Paternal command," A answered. "Isn't that right?"

"Not exactly," C said. "Choice is never easily handled, is it? And eventually, as always, it is not choice really. Rather it is given to us. The immediate response to something thudding in from the outside."

"Those Lemay bombers overhead?" B said smiling.

-§-

"Yes. There came a split second as in a flash of boom-boom and a flood of hot napalm so that flames came like driven animals cresting the suddenly rising hills before you, roaring at you—searing Jaguars spitting fire directly singeing your very face, melting your cheekbones so that you react in a direction away from the open, from their hissing, fuming mouths. Archer lurches one way, his father, his family the other and in a spectacular instant of incineration the choice has been made."

"I'll never leave Emma," Arch said quietly. "You can't make me. You're not strong enough. Not you, not Jesus, not God, not hope."

"I'll tell Emma to let you go," the pastor said and went back into the sacristy.

And at that instant detonation separated Archer from his family, flinging him beyond the street into the frying timbers of a shop of flames which chased him well away from the orange cauldron of his family's remains. In charred clothes he ran north to the hills— red-orange Jaguars chasing all the way to Lake Biwa. Only his burns and his facility with the Japanese language kept him alive until the double vaporizations of August left him to Ambassador George Atcheson's blessed deliverance.

-§-

In the sunlight B was amazed at the duplication of his walking. Yes he had made the 1200 foot soft slow ascent to the compound. And now once through the gate (C had written the code on his *meishi*) he walked down the 1200 feet to C's apartment. All that separated his going and coming was the ten foot wall topped with razor wire.

"I know it's completely absurd." C said. He was waiting in the empty car port attached to the flat. "If you had a pole vault you could have saved yourself 2400 feet of trudging."

"You're right," B said, "it's the perfect metaphor for our lives in this Elysium. Take any ordinary task and double it in ridiculous complexity. For what?"

"Japan's safety," C answered. "And besides it is our custom." He laughed.

"When it was dark I didn't mind it, but now sunlight hammers home a point. And you choose to live here."

"It's my destiny. Besides, it is our custom. So please come into it." C gestured to the steps up from the car port to his apartment. And in single file the two ascended and entered unit 114.

After Graham port had been poured and C and B were sitting at the Formica-topped faux birch table near the kitchen, C said, "I wanted you to look around carefully and designate which books you'd like. I've decided to pare down for final dissolution."

B laughed. "Cheery thought. In Japan we don't discuss such feelings, don't in fact feel them. Or if we feel them, deny them. I'm sure you know that. At some point I'll ask what the fuck you mean by dissolution but not now. After the port, maybe if I remember it."

"I just wanted you to have the chance to pick out whatever you liked."

"As a memory or an acquisition?" B laughed.

"Your preference. Your designation."

"I suppose they're linked, as doubtless you intended. How can I acquire some books of yours and not remember you?"

"Somehow I think you'll find a way. Or more likely a better distraction."

"You bet I will. I'm not going to spend much time brooding, mooning over your exit, as much as I occasionally like you."

"So it's settled. You'll take all the books on Bonhoeffer and Shostakovich."

"Hell no! I came to Japan to get free of authority—that's what it means to be *gaijin* here. You're the absolutely the same, aren't you?"

" It's true enough that if you live here long enough you realize all your beliefs about life are just contrivances in your head. And they're all brittle enough to come clatteringly down or maybe just washed away in the tsunami of *Yamatodamashi*. They're like those cars floating inland at Fukushima—silly entities of some kind of choice rendered meaningless in the rising relentless sea. I'm not sure that makes you free of authority. Does it?"

"Okay . . . Okay." B said, letting the silence grow. Relishing an extended pause was a very Japanese proclivity.

C refilled port for both, and at length said, "The Portuguese were onto something, weren't they?"

"It's good stuff."

"I got into it first when my father told me the best Communion wine was tawny port, cut with just a dollop of water."

"In Maine ours, when we had it, was always grape juice, and kind of sour tasting."

"The same in Kobe at the Union church, and then never weekly, sometimes not even monthly."

"I haven't been in a church in maybe twenty years, and despite some nice memories, I don't miss it a bit. I prefer the shrine route. Shake a bell rope, clap your hands, bow your head and think thoughts, or no thoughts, or ask for advice over some dilemma. And buy trinkets on the way out."

"So you think of some of these books as trinkets at my shrine, with rather a better price."

"Are you trying to sound posthumous? If so, I can get into it, but I'll need more port."

C refilled their glasses.

"How about some snacks?" B said. "You must have some *sembei*, some lousy crackers, don't you?"

C went into the kitchen and came back with a plate. "Are these lousy enough?"

"Not quite," B answered. "They need more aging so they can get really soggy or tired or whatever, but, they go well with the port. Do you have any mysteries? Or some light British social manners tales?"

"Maybe. You can look around."

"I suppose I'd rather do that after you're gone. I don't want to hurry things. Eighty could be the new seventy-five for you."

"I wouldn't mind being seventy-five again. I'd have two more molars on the upper right."

B pushed his chair back on the parquet floor, making a scuffing sharp noise. He then slumped back, took a visible breath.

"Okay, tell me about dissolution. Is it cancer, or just despair, or God forbid, a longing to go back to the states?"

"Some longing, but not for the states. I'd like to finish up the writing, get everything unspooled."

"I don't encourage it. Your unspooled stuff bogs down and bores most any reader."

"The caring tone of your calumny always astonishes me."

"It's my frank nature and you love it. And more importantly you need it. Without my fine tuning your stuff will never sell."

"Is it that sales have been so slow?"

"You bet . . . More port." B pushed back to the table. "When you write from experience it's boring, don't you get that?"

"I get it. I get," C said. "Women have told me that."

"They're all inscrutable, deliciously inscrutable, right up to the moment when you strangle them. It's right at that moment their fear clarifies their essence." B laughed, downed his port.

"You sound like Madame Vincouvier in full flower."

"I never went there," B said. "Should I have?"

"Maybe it's best never to have regrets." C said. "I long for a first hour that I don't have even a whit of consciousness ever. Do you understand that?"

"No."

"Can you tie your shoes now in the morning? Easily? Can you put your pants on without sitting in a chair to do it? Do you slip to the right getting out of bed and reel around getting to the bathroom? The first hour is the cruelest, the toughest, the worst of the day. The first hour, Jesus, the first hour. I hate it like it's a real vile little animal squirming out of my grip. Full sixty minutes behaving like a rabid weasel. You don't have it yet, do you? The first hour sets out tasks that nearly kill me. I shouldn't have to think about them, much less connive to achieve them, all the while chuckling at my incapacity. You don't know much about that, do you? Of course you don't. If you want to cross the room, you do so. You step into your underwear—what's to worry about doing that? What's so astonishing to accomplish that? What is? You don't know, do you? Why am I bleating like this? What could be wrong?"

"At first I thought you were talking about death, and the first hour of separation. But, hell, parts wear out," B said, smiling. "Deal with it. You're still in the game, so hit the ball back."

"Each first hour I get up thinking. It's bad now but in an hour it will be better. If I can hang on long enough the agony—well, okay, not agony—that will lessen in the next hour. The next hour will be lots better, lots easier. It's what I have to look forward to. After the first hour it's downhill, and the game can still be mine. Everything hurts, but it's the pain of a neglectful parent, maybe. Maybe not. Not a parent, just a skeptic brought in from the outside to laugh at you, in case you stop laughing at yourself."

"More port, please."

"Why should I give you more of anything? You won't even take away my books. My stupid books."

"I said I'd take the mysteries and the manners stuff. That's a kind offer. More than you deserve. Better you should stay here and end up eating your books."

"Sometimes I think eating shouldn't be so difficult. You know you start chewing something and suddenly half a tooth is mixed with it, and you probe around with your tongue to find the broken piece, the loose crown or whatever, and you know you might swallow it, but you can't really swallow that easily and you think, what the hell, you might just choke to death, and that might not be so bad. Not so bad. Do you ever wonder if you'd finish your time here by strangling? Simply choking to death on something too large to go down easily—which in fact ten years ago would have slid down without a comment or a thought?"

"Actually I don't think about strangling much. I think you should be worried about having a stroke. They come out of nowhere, totally undeserved, and the wreckage is impressive. You'd drool like a five month old baby, unable to sit up for any length of time, unable to walk or even point to something. That's what you should worry about, if you ask me."

By the time half of the port had been consumed, they moved on to a favorite topic: Japan.

"I've stopped thinking about it," B said. "It's the water I swim in. I know it instinctively now."

"Gaijin cannot," C answered. "You periodically come out of the pool and thus imagine you have perspective on the water. But you don't either. You're too long here and you know it. I bet you dream speaking English slowly. I bet you dream about personal embarrassment, about sitting eternally on a stool outside your favorite restaurant awaiting the call to vittles that never comes. Or you lie on tatami and imagine it the most inviting place on earth, afternoon sunlight baking the mats with a warmth you could sprawl across, wiggle across, slump across, with that utter safety that surrounds Japan from your baked imagination outward. Ah, silken Japan so tightly around my wrists and ankles." C said, sighing and smiling almost to silliness. Mme. Vincouvier's masked face leaned in closer, her minted breath almost fiery on his blindfold.

"The place institutionalizes our alienation." B said, "And who would have it any other way?"

"The place takes my alienation to heights no one could have imagined. No one should imagine."

B sighed, slumped and looked quizzically at C. "Am I supposed to bite on that statement? Beg for elucidation? Or simply ask Madame Vincouvier."

"She'd like to tell you, show you, experience you."

"I bet that sagging skinned sad sack would indeed. But it's not in the cards, is it? Life's too short."

"You have no idea."

"Are we back to dissolution again? Am I supposed to bite on that too? Do you have dark revelations to tell me? If so, more port, please."

"Port of entry," C said. "Or is that too obscene?"

"Who gives a fuck?"

"Madame V. knows how to spiral you out of unconsciousness. Japan only knows how to build unconsciousness. Japan and America through the same lulling process of endless entertainment in ever more compressed and portable items and terms. Both places determined to hammer you into non-existence and ultimate self-laceration. Needles through your tongue up through and out of your eyes."

Half way through the second bottle of port B and C were locked in a fellow feeling, bonhomie that left time for long silences as the dusty grey sky turned darker through the filmy white window liners.

C said, "Two old men at a Formica- slick table as the day dies, just as surely as they die with it."

"I'm not," B answered. "And I don't have to be whipped into action, into caring."

"When you hit bottom, Mme V. will be there ready to lift you."

"Jesus. I'm not that far gone."

"I'm ten years ahead of you in that regard. And ready and happy for any lifting, any at all." C took a long swallow of port, and then said, "Why not take all of my books. I'm not going to read them again. And Japanese students tell me they're only good as pillows."

"You're not off- loading your detritus on me. Give them to Mme V., in return for skipping the hot wax."

"You never want to skip the hot wax. It wakes up blood left in a coma decades ago."

"My blood is as fresh as a daisy."

"A snuffed Daisy, God rest her bloated soul."

"Jesus I'd forgotten about her. I wonder what they gave her. What's the potion that iced her in less than a minute? Might be nice to have it on hand."

"For those too-*gaijin*-for-any-gaijin moments? When you or they speak too quickly and communication vanishes like wind over grass?"

"Such a fucking poet."

"It was Biblical . . . or maybe those moments when Japan's warmth and softness lets you out of history. Sets you floating awash in genial warmth and minute esthetic delight so that each second is wholly contained, pearl shaped, and savored as if a pearl itself, when you feel subsumed in a sweet silent escalator heading upwards at the speed you wish it, when you wish it, and everyone beside you in equivalent lift-off. Sake soaked lift-off. Nothing sweeter, all desire transcended, and pillowed liberation experienced so deeply as to be beyond communication, just perfectly sensed. Cloud throttling, and release from caring— such soft release like listening to a gate unlatching underwater."

"Getting out of history—that would be worth investment, wouldn't it? Fucking A! That's what I say. Unplug me and start over. It would be like lingering at that moment just before you come when there's no stopping no lingering even as you long to linger. A glorious disembowelment. You can hear the delicious sound of adhesive pulling your innards away from whatever sheathing exists wherever it might exist."

"Yes, straining against the collar. Near asphyxiation and yet beyond history."

"A statement that says you're either a Buddhist or a simple S & M freak. Which is it?"

"I'm my Daddy's boy. Check the Buddhist box."

"I remember hearing you hated Daddy. You get only a light pencil marking."

"In life, as well as in your stupid charting."

"With cessation of desire, so the cessation of suffering, or unsatisfactoriness."

"Ah, nicely learned. Persuasive and vapid, vapid and persuasive. You're very essence. In desperate need of sharpening. Honing to the point you might deserve my books. So here's a story you need to digest, absorb, interiorly mull over in thinking about me." C pulled a manila envelope from the bookcase behind the Formica table and handed it to B.

"Oh shit! I can't read it now. I'm too blissful to read your maunderings."

C said, "Oh, but you have too. It's an essential part of Archer's story."

The Riches of This World, Part F

(Passion in Pusan)

Young Archer, already flattened and grieving over Ambassador George Atcheson's accidental death in the Pacific, stalwartly continued (in what he knew was a zombie existence) with his translation duties, allowing them to drift into more mundane areas — preparing Japanese versions of various regulations coming from Supreme Command. Explaining various Japanese publications back to Supreme Command to buttress their escalating sense of infallibility and worship from all local populations. He understood vaguely that it was only his services to Atcheson that had prevented him from reassignment to stateside duty or perhaps to base work in Okinawa or the Philippines. Supreme Command by the fall of 1948 was not interested in further development of data concerning Ishii's atrocities at Unit 731. Green Cross had been formed and reabsorbed most of the young doctors who been such avid experimenters in Manchuria. Ishii himself was untouched by the war crimes accusations. He rested comfortably in Tokyo, lionized as a brilliant son of Japan who had performed crucial research in water purification in Harbin. So long as Ishii shared incrementally his findings, the Americans, it became clear, were more than willing to let him flourish in post war Japan. His weaponizing of disease justified his continuing protection by the morally compromised occupiers of Japan. Archer's colleague, Atushi Sumi was particularly offended by Ishii's golden situation, but Archer himself dizzy from his family's incineration, and now Atcheson's inexplicable accident, thought Sumi's passion was more than misplaced, in truth ridiculous. In the riot of death and chaos the war had unleashed how could anyone be outraged? What was outrage in the face of mass vaporization? If the Americans could snuff 100,000 lives in less than ten seconds, how could one find the spread of glanders, cholera, or anthrax throughout the Manchurian populations, or the occasional vivisection of hapless human subjects (Ishii's doctors referred to them as 'logs'), how could you be outraged by such activities? Against the war's slaughter, how could you measure the calculated butchery of a few thousand Chinese prisoners? What would Jesus have said?

So Archer kept his translation duties at the top of consciousness and before his superiors as necessary aids to their continuing occupation success. But even as Archer maximized his usefulness he fell more deeply into embarrassed disconnection from everything going on in Tokyo. SCAP knew what it was doing or thought it did; Archer expedited those feelings by translating those messages to Japanese underlings who carried out SCAP's directives. But the images of atrocity contained in 731's notes surfaced every time Archer tried to find the proper Japanese verb to suggest which democratic process properly fit Japanese culture, or, more prosaically, which verb captured step 6 of cleaning a western style toilet. Bureaucratise undermined Archer's sense of moral judgment. And he knew after a year of trivial translation that he must escape somehow, even if it meant leaving the Armed Service, that savior of his soul. He spent another year exploring options as the overall enrollment in the Army drew down. Sumi had left to return to his *furosato* to attend to whatever relatives had survived the endless bombing. And without Sumi Archer's instinct to find something worthwhile in his efforts diminished. At length he spent more and more time pouring over openings elsewhere in Asia, even after enough despair, in America itself.

The war in Korea ended his explorations. Abruptly he found a way to mobilize himself directly into the initial phases of that losing enterprise. But he carefully orchestrated his obligations to keep him from direct action—no small feat since the initial phase of the war tossed American bodies against a tough charging enemy who easily overran South Korea, reducing allied resistance to a desperate foothold on the peninsula around Pusan harbor. For a brief interval it seemed Archer's assignment to "body shipments" away from the front line would not be sufficient to keep him out of combat. The front lines threatened to reach the docks where Archer wrapped young American corpses in white plastic sheets for flights back to the states. But if that assignment was to liberate him from the horrors of 731 it proved a bust. Blasted bodies of 20 year olds, intestines flowing out of perforated corpses, brains spilling along smooth cheek bones, missing feet, grotesquely burned backs, flayed legs, eyeless sockets only underscored the truism that warfare could easily and automatically exceed experimentation in hideousness. How get free of memory in the midst of daily swathing of atrocities? Archer looked for salvation in *soju* at small bars or canteens. And just when he began truly to envy Atcheson's watery grave, just as he longed to join him in the ocean of remorse rejecting all rescue or perhaps tugged under by conspirators from Green Cross or SCAP itself, just at that moment when it seemed he had swallowed a vat of kimchi, Ginny materialized.

Ginny took him firmly in hand and with the softest southern accent from her small beak like mouth guided him out of desperation and loneliness's long slide. She was eight years older, generations wiser, in every way more substantial than Archer. She outweighed him. Their only mutual interests, at least initially, were *soju*, and Korean phonetic writing, and pornography.

"You sound the words almost perfectly but I can tell you have no idea what the sounds mean. Isn't that so?" she said two stools away at the bar of "Ralph's Canteen."

Archer was startled that she addressed him. He tried to remember what she looked like, but didn't want to turn toward her. Plump but surely not fat. "I can connect the sounds to what I need."

"Limited needs, I gather," she said.

"Elemental ones," he answered.

"We all have those."

"Should I move a stool over?"

"Why don't you?"

He stood up, turned toward her, studied carefully. A rush of interest and nascent excitement made him awkward moving to the next stool. He had trouble getting his right buttock situated. "Japanese women cover their mouths and whinny to show interest. I like your American approach," he said.

"Loneliness has its desperations," she answered.

"That's me, Mr. Cure-Your-Loneliness."

"How come you know about Japanese women?"

"I lived there all of my life till now."

"I'm from Tennessee."

They talked about her upbringing. She taught 3rd grade at a Base school. He wrapped dead bodies for shipment. "We deserve each other," she said.

"I don't deserve anybody," he answered.

"Ah, listen to you, so sorry for yourself. A whiner, why don't you cover your mouth with your dainty hand?"

"You have a nasty way about you."

"You bet. You can't soften my edges."

Archer recalled turning five photographs over in Atcheson's stunned presence: five pictures of a woman enduring a Caesarian without anesthesia and then deliberately disemboweled while the baby rested beside her on the gurney. "Useful battlefield research," Archer had said, while Atcheson turned from the photos and stared at him in apparent amazement, taking sharper breaths. "A different kind of study for water purification," Archer had continued. "First rate inquiry, the kind Nobel Prize winners undertake."

"Jesus," Atcheson had replied, slumping back in his leather tilting chair. "Jesus! And we welcome them home . . . Jesus."

"I've been in the middle of some . . . some intelligence stuff. Pretty horrible," Archer said wondering if his solemn tone was the correct approach. Wasn't everything horrible . . . horrible with unsoft edges?

"I was married almost eight years," she answered matter of factly, "to Earl the abuser. That's why I'm here. So we're not so different." She added a quick, clicking laugh. "And the Heineken costs only a quarter."

"If it's not dime night," he added.

"When's that?"

"Wednesdays, and packed."

"Let's not do that."

"It's a date." They switched to *soju*.

Later in her third storey cinder block studio they drank a full liter of *soju* and she showed him a small flat magazine of pornography. There was a black and white photo of a penguin shaped naked fellow with his erect penis and tightened scrotum resting on a white dinner plate—probably fairly cold, Archer thought. A naked woman was holding a knife and fork over the plate.

"Want to try that?" Ginny said giggling.

-§-

B took a winnowing breath and looked up from the manuscript. "Is this preparation, or maybe explanation for Mme Vincouvier?"

C smiled and opened a third bottle of tawny port. "I hadn't thought of that. Mme. Vincouvier is real. Ginny's just a story."

"A rather more interesting one. What happens next?"

"Oral sex."

-§-

"Earl was not much interested. If you know what I mean." Ginny said.

"You mean he was interested enough receiving but not giving. . . I'm not Earl."

"Good enough," she said, turning the page. "Let's try this." The penguin fellow was sitting on a chair; the woman was inverted, her shoulders resting on his knees; her knees on his shoulders, their mouths lapping and sucking genitals. Archer mouthing dark moistness, jerked upwards at her nips but nonetheless before and during ejaculation conjured the slow uncoiling lines of pus from the "log's" induced glanders, and then arterial spurts of blood from a "controlled" experiment of deliberate femoral slashing.

"Did you enjoy it?" she asked tentatively with a tenderness and solicitation Archer had not much encountered.

"You know I did, nearly gagging you."

"I thought it was painful for you."

"Stop playing Florence Nightingale."

"I know what I know."

Archer said from a quietness and concern he didn't expect, "Well, I'm glad you know what you know. That's more than what I know."

"I know enough to listen to my mama when she said, 'get away from Earl. I don't care how you have to do it, but just do it.' And I did. He was trash, dirty, smelly trash."

"I didn't know him."

"Count your blessings. My mama said 'you get away. On your own. Just get away."

"And here we are in Pusan, Korea, about as far away as you can get from where?"

"East Kentucky. Earl's country, but I got away all right."

"I suppose he hit you."

"One time with a coke bottle, right after we got married. He was trash. And mean. Mean as a snake. I put restraining on him, but didn't make any difference. Before it could be served, just as soon as he heard about—and he had friends from high school in the police. Just as soon as he heard about it, he came right over and busted me in the mouth. I had to get new teeth. Two new teeth. I can take them out. He cost me the best job I ever had, teaching third grade. He came by the school, cursing me out, cursing so they had to get the police to come haul him away. And the principal said he couldn't keep me on, given the 'marital baggage' I had. I loved that. 'Marital baggage' that surely described Earl. 'Marital baggage.' Jesus!"

As he listened Archer turned over in his mind the question whether atrocity could be arranged in a hierarchy. Did experiments in Harbin, only known through slow translation, rank above or below Ginny's life stories? And in their extensive sampling of the little black and white magazine's many illustrative pages it seemed she could add yet another astonishing memory to match his plunge over orgasm's crumbling mica edge.

At the end of a week of bondage exploration she told him. "The only job I could get after Earl wrecked the third grade. All I could get was a kind of nurse's aide to St. George's mini hospital. Everybody called him Saint George and maybe he was a saint. Maybe. You see he'd gotten a write up in our weekly, *The Sentinel*, about his saintly work bringing maimed children out of Vietnam for rehabilitation in America, at a local Shriner's burn hospital in Lexington, or at the university medical facility. And the kids he brought out were in terrible shape. Okay? Terrible, burned or amputated limbs of bent spines. After the French gave up, he could go to Saigon or even to Hanoi and find kids left behind from the war and in terrible condition and bring them to Kentucky for treatment. And of course their parents lined up to get his help. It didn't cost them anything, though probably he took what he could to cover his expenses, flying in and all. He didn't pay for the treatment, or maybe he did at the start but pretty soon, doctors and hospitals volunteered to help out, and he kept finding kids and he said finally he could not finish interviewing potential patients because the minute word got out he was in town, lines formed. I think it had something to do with Asian religion—you know thinking whatever happened happened because of something you didn't do or did badly in a previous life. So it was better to hide your disabled kid. That was better than showing you walked around with bad karma or whatever. Lot of shame in that I guess. But it wasn't like St. George had to go beating the bushes for patients. The bushes came screaming to him. And when he got the kids into Kentucky, lots of churches, doctors, lawyers even, signed up to help St. George do God's work. It was, I assure you, God's work. The kids were malnourished, sickly thin. And St. George fattened them up, with special milk shakes full of nutrients. I had to make them every morning. Also two other nurses. And then we had to take them to their treatment centers, then back to the duplex St. George had inherited from his parents. And St. George himself was sort of crippled. One bad leg left over from polio when he was young. He spent a lot of time with his kids, as he called them. They were his whole life. He put an addition onto the duplex so he could bring more over. I never understood how he got through customs or visas, but I suppose all he had to do was show them maimed kids and the doors opened, especially if churches and officials sanctioned what he was doing. And they did. Did they ever! St. George."

Archer said, "You sound skeptical. Are you?"

"Maybe. Sometimes I'd notice St. George cuddling with his kids, and I'd get a creepy feeling. Maybe I'm a creepy myself."

"No question about that." Archer said, smiling. "We're exploring the far edge of creepy."

Then they'd turn a page in the porn magazine.

After a long session with mirrors, Archer asked, "Why did you leave St. George or were you let go?"

"No. Earl found where I was and he came 'round. At first polite as all that, asking how I was doing and if St. George needed anything. But I could tell it was only a ruse. Soon enough he'd be back demanding I go with him, kowtow to him like before. And it would be sick again and smelly and trashy, and I'd have to be rid of it. So I started talking with the Army. I figured if I got in they'd keep him out. He couldn't get on the base, could he? Better yet they said they needed teachers on bases in Korea, and Korea they said was "a helluva long way from here." That's what they said. And Earl couldn't get there, could he?"

"Do you think Earl was settling your life?"

"Getting rid of him surely was. And also getting rid of St. George. I think I was seeing more things than I should have."

"Between George and his patients?"

"Maybe. It was creepy. Creepy because what I was thinking about St. George. Creepy, maybe, for those kids—"

"But they were getting help. Their lives were improving. And that probably was an easy trade-off for them, don't you think. Nutrition and pain relief in return for what? Sad cuddling? Real care and not phony imagined parental care?"

"Maybe something worse," Ginny said.

"You don't know. You never saw anything, did you?"

"No."

"I didn't either. Not directly but I saw evidence."

"Could you get evidence?"

"I didn't want to."

"Of course. That would have forced you to believe the worst and you didn't want to, did you?"

"I surely didn't."

"So leave it at that. You didn't see any. I saw plenty but I didn't want to see it, or do anything about it. Ambassador Atcheson did. Did he ever! And He got dead because of it."

"Dead?"

"Oh, it was ruled an accident. His plane crashed in the Pacific. He drowned. Most others were rescued. They never got his body — not ever. "

"Where?"

"Not so far from Hawaii"

"Could he have swum there?'

Archer laughed—"A 50-mile swim. Takes a while. Sharks. They never found anything. No life preservers. Nothing."

Outside, noise from a rolling barrel. Rapid fire Korean shouting, then silence.

Ginny said, shifting in sagging coils of the bed so that creaking muffled the shouts, "I worry about those kids — what were they thinking about when he cuddled them, held them on his lap."

-§-

Looking up from the story, B said, "And so Archer and Ginny live happily ever after, having found such wondrous sexual compatibility, such slurping energy? Such mutual delights?"

"Hardly," C answers. "They split up just as the Korean Armistice is being negotiated.

"Under what circumstances?" B asks.

"I'm working on that still. Would be interesting, if Earl showed up in Korea?"

"Might be lively at least. Who knows it might be nice if he turned up lively and likable. Your characters are not very likable."

"Earl is not likable. And he does not turn up in Korea. Suffice it to say Ginny leaves."

"You have to supply a reason. You have to."

"No, I don't. You can supply your own."

"I refuse. I absolutely refuse. You must have written something, outlined something. I'm holding two more pages. What's on them?"

"Nothing of value. Ginny leaves. Perhaps she's pregnant or believes so. Perhaps her mother dies in Kentucky. Perhaps Earl has a come-to-Jesus moment and summons her home with a telling apology. More likely she loses her job teaching at the base, or is hospitalized and contracts an infection that Asian medicine cannot cure. Shortly after breakup, Archer himself leaves Asia and returns to California for a decade of debauchery. It's a really hateful interval riddled with selfishness and psychedelic drugs. He pretends to be a Presbyterian Missionary returning to the homeland to heal the trauma of his incinerated family, his beloved family. He parlays that story into a myriad of home stays among the faithful until the drugs flash removal, and hence onto the next consoling household. He gets near endless mileage out of recounting the atrocities he had to minutely translate, minutely document for an American ambassador literally at war with his superiors over America's cooperation with Japanese hideous butchers in return for the details of their data. He gets to expedite the re-integration of killers into Japanese society as esteemed scientists whose only sin was patriotism, diligence, and meticulous record-keeping. So lovingly does he relive each atrocity with its attendant self-horror that whatever tension his addiction might occasion is immediately washed away in righteous syncopation of fellow feeling. Christ speaks through him toward the coming kingdom of compassion notched more vividly by brandy, mescaline, peyote, heroin, meth, and chocolated cherries. Then just before final collapse he gets a wondrous house-sit in the idyllic hill country of Southern California and there among hanging bougainvillea and tea farms and daily perfect weather he finds a perfect bottom, the purest sludge of despair. Lying on thick camel's hair carpeting he watches the sun retreat among the rows of tea trees, listens to the endless cicada clicking, imagines but never sees, the dread *mukade* centipedes of his youthful terror in rural Japan and finally succumbs to a finishing cocktail of booze and heroin that somehow catapults him into a miserable pink painted concrete rehab unit in downtown Escondito where he meets Jenna and weds deliverance. Enough summary?"

"Not really. I need to know a good deal more about his deliverance. It's too pat in summary."

"Read the play." C said, handing over a three ring notebook with cover picturing a streaking *shinkansen* before a distant, yet gleaming, Mt. Fuji.

The Riches of This World, Part G

(A Play in 2 Scenes)

The curtain opens revealing a large room with sparkling pink-tinted cinder block walls holding five Styrofoam- white, square 3 foot tables with four white folding chairs at each. A table at the extreme left and right each has four elderly male occupants holding apparently intense conversations without vocalizing. The table at center stage has only one occupant, Archer, slumped over head resting on the table top and eyes closed. He is unshaven (at least a week) wearing a filthy white Guayabera long sleeve shirt, and jeans, no shoes, grey tattered socks. From stage right a young woman, Jenna, (probably 17 or 18 years old) with blond hair enters. She wears jeans and a maroon tank top; she carries a Lucite pitcher full of water and ice and quickly comes to Archer's table.

Jenna: Heads up! You need your water. What did I tell you? Water is essential if you want the leg cramps to subside. That's a fact, a pure fact. Ask any physician. Wake up. Heads up. Time to drink. [She places a clear plastic cup on the table top, slowly pours out a drink]. You need this. Drink this up, Hess, drink it up for mama. The Holy Spirit says, Drink Up!

[Archer lifts his head few inches, moans and slumps again. Jenna pours the water on his head, a slow thin strip of wetness.]

Archer: Jesus!

Jenna: You are not permitted to curse here. You know that.

Archer: Jesus!

Jenna: Think of it as a kind of baptism. Escondido righteousness. The Holy Spirit transforming you. The new you. Righteous, Hess—what a gift to the world! Drink in the Holy Spirit. Come on, four good sips or more on your head. Got it?

Archer: Okay! I got it. Stop the water. I got it. I got it. [And what he got was the revelation that she was spirited and quite beautiful, with a healthy buoyancy that seemed to him to surround her lithe figure like a nimbus of good feeling. By what happenstance should it be he had come in the presence of such a creature? After taking three long sips from the plastic cup she had poured, he suddenly felt the need to vomit, and did so, tossing a vague orange stream across the table top. Were there tinges of blood in the slimy product? Instantly he felt profoundly embarrassed—a brand new feeling for him. Could it be that somehow he had done something to shame himself before her? What might that be? What sort of feeling could that generate?]

"I'm so sorry," he muttered, clamping his left arm at the edge of vomit pool to prevent its reaching the floor. "I'm so sorry," repeated and more embarrassing still found himself suddenly sobbing, crying and weirdly moaning, aware that he voice sounded strangely soothing, curling care around his shame-fear-spasms. "Oh God, I'm so sorry."

"Of course you are, Hess. It's a smelly mess, isn't it?"

His head flopped back down on the table top and the pool smelled piquant, enveloping, but as he closed his eyes against the shifting stench he imagined some kind of contamination had flooded out of him. Images from Ishii's meticulous notes seemed to dance on the pool. His blood and theirs, his puke and theirs, his bafflement and Atcheson's outrage, Sumi's disgust and his own distancing, all of it being slowly pulled out of his highly resistant intestines.

Jenna: [spraying something from a large clear plastic bottle] A little water and vinegar to rid of us of your deed. There! There! No need to fret. No need to sob. It happens. It's expected. No one escapes such easy purification. [She pulls him into an upright, sitting position, and then mops the table top with a large white towel.]

Archer: You come fully equipped.

Jenna: Endowed. Get it right!

Archer: [slowly as if digesting the phrase] En . . . dowed. Yes, indeed!

Jenna: I don't think we understand each other.

Archer: No! I understand you perfectly. See you perfectly. You are angelic. Come to bear me away, haven't you? To some better place, maybe up in the hills? Could that be it? In the hills. In the hills. Bear me away. Oh God, bear me away."

Jenna: I can see your unhappiness. [She pets the back of his head.]

-§-

B looks up from his reading, "Okay. It's just the beginning. I get that. But something's got to happen, some little narrative hook to keep my attention. It seems like you're wallowing, or better yet, bouncing on a low spring board. Always preparing for a dive, but never getting into the water. You're just bouncing up and down. You gotta get into the pool. Don't ya?

"Undoubtedly," C answered.

"So what's the purpose? How do we get to the meat?"

"Showing how Archer is quite mesmerized by meeting Jenna. Hypnotized, enchanted, bewitched, maybe. Struck dead dumb suddenly at his own vapidity, his opaque solitariness. In the presence of riotous, pursed-lipped pride that such a beauty would show even the slightest interest in his wrecked life. Skip ten pages and get to their conversation in her bedroom."

"Ah, a bedroom scene. At last!"

"You'll be disappointed. Mme Vincouvier surely was."

"You share your precious prose with her?"

"The very least of what we share."

"Oh come on! Give up the funning. No teasing. Not now. We'll doubtless never see each other again. If you go forward in this bogus return to your native land, the chances you'll return are almost nil, aren't they? More fundamentally they won't let you return. Once you've turned your back on Elysium, Elysium closes down. Besides how in hell did you get in in the first place? Was it a missionary visa? I don't think so. "

"I've seen Fuji too often from the train. We all come back, don't we? Can't really leave, can we? Just can't stay either." C said. "Living here means skipping over parts of the narrative, doesn't it? That's the blessing of the place. Anyone will happily summarize whatever you didn't have time to experience, including the best and worst moments. So skip a few pages and learn more about their relationship."

"I don't care squat about their relationship. He seems a pretty weird cripple. He'll only mess up her life."

"She saves him."

"No woman does that."

"Jenna does that. Follow along. Maybe you'll learn something."

"You're so romantic, and boring."

"But there's great animal sex in the next scenes."

"Now you're talking," B said, taking a long swallow of port. "Do I need tissues, or maybe one of those *ofuro* thin towels?"

"Only the broken tissues of your heart."

The Riches of This World, Part G, continued.

The scene takes place in the small bedroom given to Archer. They sit on the thin mattress of a narrow single bed, ticking showing beneath the fully zipped sleeping bag on top of the bed. On the wall at the head of the bed (slanted outwardly toward stage left) hangs a bronze crucifix approximately twenty inches high. On the opposite wall at the end of the bed (again slanted outwardly toward stage right) is a picture (apparently a photograph) of the Virgin Mary. Seated on the bed is Archer, his hands hiding his face, his legs over the edge of the mattress and touching the floor. Next to him is Jenna clad only in a blue/white *yukata,* partially open to reveal a good bit of her left breast. Archer is exclaiming through his clamped hands.

Archer: I always discounted stuff about the apocalypse, about the end times, about the end of recorded history, as if there would be a cataclysmic disjunction to history and God descending in a flash of judgment.. I knew that never would happen, couldn't happen although everyone had been expecting it. Dreaming about it, hunting for it, planning for it, preparing for it, summoning it as if it would wash away our sins and longings. At first my father was peerless describing it. Relishing it, or maybe just relishing its effects on his parishioners. No, it wouldn't occur. Of course it couldn't occur. Shouldn't occur. And just as I could laugh it out of consciousness, put it away forever. Just as certainly I had flushed it away, then suddenly it became blindingly clear. Of course it would happen, it did constantly happen. It was happening every day. Apocalypse every second of ever day of every week, of every moment of awareness, because end times were absolutely certain—just on an individual level. That's all it was. So evident, so obvious. For you little Archer, end times would occur at the third Thursday of June in the year you had counted on passing through. In a tough instant you suddenly understood it. Apocalypse for all, every second of every day. Pretty obvious, don't you think? Biblical fools thought it would happen to all, and it did, but separately. Pretty obvious. Don't you think?

Jenna: We all die, that's for sure.

Archer: And therefore the world ends. It's so obvious, despite lambs and flames and thrones and collected armies awaiting Armageddon. Of course the world ends. Just like that. Decapitation. It's so obvious. But that's not what I'm telling you.

Jenna: But you are, and rather at length.

Archer: No! I'm telling you this only as introduction to a better perception, a better Biblical reading. There is resurrection in precisely the same way there is true apocalypse. You only have to understand it accurately. Of course the world ends individually. Could that be the case with resurrection? Could it be daily? And only individually? The temple's curtain tearing every day at 3 p.m.? The rock rolling away every early morning just before sunrise? Why not? Well, you'd have to have a better explanation, a better rationale for such an assertion, wouldn't you? And to get one you'd have to ask every 11 year old boy with a sawed off arm in a tank of freezing water in a Mongolian plain wheezing through weather below minus forty degrees—slowly melting into oblivion congealing into brittle human ice, or every *maruta* slowly experiencing evisceration sans anesthesia . . . ask each one. But they couldn't hear your question, much less answer it. But there is resurrection. There is because I know it. Know it.

Jenna: Archer . . . Archer [she reaches over to take hold of him]

Archer: I know it because you've shown it to me. You have . . . It's possible still to be mistaken for the gardener. It is. Possible to be ghostly, an apparition of what you were, but still in need of food. To be dead and come alive. Yes, it's possible. You've shown me how. You have.

Jenna: It's all about you, isn't it?

Archer: That's not fair. I'm revealing how extraordinarily much you mean to me, how life giving you've been for me, how you've revived my sunken self, my tarred body to something like life. Something like optimism.

Jenna: The all-seeing prism of yourself. The largest, most majestic eye. Nothing scary here. Not a thing. Just dust, ashes. Dust and ashes. Nothing I did made any difference. I know you believe that. Your deliverance — out of my hands.

Archer: No. Into your hands. Your hands. [They embrace and rather awkwardly open the flap of the sleeping bag and clamber inside, kissing deeply and entwining as the lights go down.

Almost immediately the lights come back up and sitting up Archer starts to pontificate.]

Archer: Sometimes I think it would have been so great to take you to meet my parents—not so much Emma but my parents. How your radiance would have astonished them, unbalanced them. I can hear my father rasply whispering about desire's linkage to suffering and reminding me, always reminding me, of the necessity to transcend fleshy delights. He might never understand how wet we get, how furiously we slip inside each other and spiral and spiral— spiral toward some delicious mind-bending deliverance. He'd be muttering koans and striking meditative poses, furiously listening to the pulsating throb his own inflammations. Screaming quietly self-repudiating aphorisms of control and dissolution. We should take him in here with us [Archer holds up one flap of the sleeping bag]. Good Christ, we'd never find him again. He'd never come out! [As the lights dim, Archer and Jenna clamber back into the sleeping bag and in the enveloping darkness, Archer shouts/laughs.]

Archer: And on the third day he rose again . . .

-§-

B stopped reading the draft and said, "Phony manipulative stuff. Not quite we'd hoped for, is it?"

"And what did we hope for?" C said, smiling.

"Better gymnastics," B answered. "And with the lights on, in full view."

"You're Shinjuku mind," C said.

"Yours too! But you're too afraid to let it fall open."

"I am not afraid."

"Good for you, but I'm not seeing it. Surely not reading it."

"Fill in the blanks. Tighten your *fundoshi* and wade in. Or are you too afraid of resurrection? Think of that shimmering, ghostly presence going on forever. For. . . ever. Endless shimmering in soft blue sky, hairless flesh leaping all about. It might be better, more interesting, to eviscerate *maruta*. Killing more interesting than joyous tedium? Torturing more fun than ejaculating? Come tell me, vaunted night manager of the VW world." C said.

"You're beginning to sound like Archer."

"And why not? I made him up."

"And so poorly formed . . . "

"Yes, occasionally grotesque."

"So clearly, not you. And you can say how it all turns out. What sweetness in life they had beyond their *umami* sleeping bag in a ticking lined universe. Did it last, his resurrection? Did they marry? Were there children?"

"A daughter."

"Jesus, Hesseltine's daughter . . . All that drugging and still she was spawned without gills?"

"Gills of another sort."

"And you know how it comes out?"

"What comes out?"

"Their life together. How does it go? Are they winners? Tops on the best salesperson's listings?"

"You've seen them so happy together, surviving, indeed thriving in the great earthquake and guiding hapless Owen out of his theodicy thicket."

"I suppose I remember that. I suppose. But what about them now? How are they doing? Any better than we're doing—swilling port and listening to ligaments shred, tendons droop or sever, and skin dry up toward cracking?"

"I've written one ending, but I don't know for whom it applies."

"Do I get to see it?"

"You're actually interested?"

"How long is it?"

"Too long. And not yet very clear. Just sort of suggestive."

"Plausible?"

"Yes."

"Oh all right, I'll take it along. I'll read it when I have more energy, maybe. Maybe."

C left the living room and sprinted up the stairs to his study. Presently he came back down holding a manila folder. "After you've read it, you'll have to tell me who it applies to. I really don't know. I knew once but things have gotten fuzzy lately."

"Yes, haven't they?"

"Promise you'll pass it along. A might actually like to read it."

"Oh, at some point—admittedly distant and now not quite discernable—I'll probably enjoy it too."

"It comes with a price. You have to take it with the books, all the books."

"I never contracted for all the books, only a few."

"Yes, I remember now. Only Bonhoeffer and Shostakovich—birds of a feather—bookends of some larger story perhaps."

"How coy! Give me the folder, and let me rest a while before trudging back that absurd route. Anyone needs sleep before your prose."

V: A, B, C, David Moran

C says, "Before you can appreciate—perhaps that's too loaded a word—before you can grasp these next stories, you need to review the first two volumes of this quartet."

"I didn't read them. Just tell me what I need to know to get ahold of what's happening."

"That's a pretty tall order. You want me to summarize two books in a couple of paragraphs"

"You could leak over to three paragraphs, if it's really necessary. But I have faith in you. Not so much faith in your turgid prose, but in you to reveal what I need to know, to. . . to appreciate, (to use your word) what you have written. So, give it a shot. Work at it. Take the challenge. You might surprise yourself."

"The real surprise would be getting you to read the first two books, but since that didn't and doubtless won't happen, I'll tell you about Prof. David Moran. He makes a lucky connection and lands the task of writing a biography of a U.S. diplomat who seems to share elite status or at least elite entry into celebrity politics, as well as celebrity publishing. So his popular ascent is chronicled, but more important for him is his collapsing relationship with his much younger wife, Natalie. She seems to have a penetrating grasp of his deficiencies and at the same time a paralyzing sadness about their life together. At its best the two books detail academic and marital combat, the one feeding off the other—disciplines and disciples. Moran unlike present company didn't opt for cross cultural marriage that so magically transcends the natural antagonisms of men and women." C smiles at his companions. "The first three volumes spend perhaps too much time on Moran's slow grasp of Japanese atrocities during World War II—in particular the experiments carried out in Harbin, Manchuria under the banner of water purification at Unit 731. Moran rides a double-hump camel to desperation: one hump of unfathomable human savagery, the other of a marital desecration he simply cannot perceive even after implosion. So what I'm giving to you is a story of Moran's earliest days of marriage, and then a much later moment of achievement and obliteration. You can grieve or not as you like. I don't think either will change your behaviors."

A remarks, "How can we thank you enough?"

The Riches of This World, Part H

(A Story Inconceivable Today, But In Its Time So Very Sweet)

For an instant Moran imagined she had decided not to get in. Then a bronze Buick Riviera went around his waiting Datsun, and she opened the door.

"I'm going to the High School," she said, eyes clear, innocent, mesmerizing.

"I take 117," Moran countered. Her straight hair hung down to the old black vinyl of the passenger seat.

"Great! You go right by it." She climbed in, slammed the too light door.

Moran eased back onto the macadam. "You're late?"

"Yes, and I have a biology test too."

"Missed the bus?"

"Of course!"

"You can't be too late."

"Well, we've about exhausted that line," Moran said looking at her, hoping to catch the soft clear eyes.

She didn't answer, only extended her jeaned legs, pushed the dirty white sneakers against his black carpeting on the firewall. Her face was incredibly oval and soft, Moran thought. The lips weren't quite right. From the side they resembled a beak, but a soft beak. Flesh owl with clear, innocent grey-green eyes. Owls ate mice he remembered.

"How big is the high school?"

"Oh, about 2000 kids."

"That's pretty big. You like it?"

She turned to him. He expected a flip remark, something from a T.V. show along the lines of why don't you just drive along, huh? He actually braced for young but knowledgeable grasp of his calculated inquiry.

"Oh yes, I do. It's a great place. Really is. It's so much better than Junior High. No bells. I mean you can do what you want when you want. Flexible learning. Your own module. I have all kinds of free time. Today my classes are over at noon. I'm a sophomore and transition is like day and night. Day and night. I mean the difference. I love it. In Junior High you never had any of your own time."

"You're a sophomore?"

"Yes."

Moran thought, how old are sophomores? She seemed tall for a sophomore. They waited for a commuter train to leave the station in Lincoln—two dirty silver coaches behind a bobbing yellow board.

"It's a regional high school then?" Moran said.

"Yes, the whole district."

"And you really like it?"

"Of course! It's great, really great."

When they were beyond the station—scrub autumn browns lining 117 rushing by, Moran said, "I'm interested that you like. I'm a teacher myself—"

"Not at Darcy!"

"No, in Worcester—actually a professor history."

She had turned back and was staring out the window.

"My college," Moran went on "is innovating. Is it the flexibility that makes you like it?"

They passed a pond brownish grey in mid-November's sunlight. "What I mean is that we're very interested in raising the motivation of our students. We've been implementing quite a number of changes, getting, incidentally, a good bit of grant money for the changes, and if you had perceptions on the—"

"You drive to Worcester every day?"

"Yes."

"Why don't you live there?"

"My wife goes to graduate school. We live in Cambridge. It's easier for me to commute."

"Every day?"

"Well, four days a week anyway."

"Long way."

"Not so bad. It's a pleasant ride. I enjoy the company."

She brought her sneakers back tucking them under the seat. "The best change to make," she said they crossed an old stone bridge over brown marshes, "is the lockers. Replace the metal lockers with plastic ones. That really helps. Really helps. No slamming around. No banging. Just a nice soft click. It's really great."

In his eleven o'clock lecture Moran said, "Clarence Gauss moved upstairs in the Embassy to a tiny attic as if, I like to think, to shelter himself from the churning diplomatic currents below. First into the attic and then across the street, across the clattering street to be away from the constant changes. Perhaps to develop perspective. More likely to insulate himself from the younger men of the Embassy who by their expertise naturally took policy making out of his hands. Was Gauss discouraged? Most assuredly, though no dispatches, naturally enough, directly state that." It occurred to Moran as he droned on that no particular point had been made. These strange investigations of motivation kept coming into his lectures, especially as Moran's biography of Gauss progressed through the second draft.

Moran covered how foxy Roosevelt kept Gauss always in an attic or across a street from real policy decisions. What did Gauss find in the attic? An oval face?

On the drive back into Cambridge Moran was ecstatic. She filled the empty seat and the soft sophomore voice was alive in the Datsun interior, and the sky was an enormous blue, clear stark blue—leafless trees etched into it. White colonial demi-mansions chipped out of it. The magic swirl of still violet brown red leaves hurled faience tossed upward as if to re-grasp their branches. The ponds' rippled, blue-doppling chrome then stretched over all walls in chill streams through his throat, mind, heart. He fairly bounced in the bucket seat.

"Notice," he explained to her clear, soft image, "the following ad, the French accent in particular. Notice the artificially heavy

French accent, 'Fronkly I could not believe suzh wine existed out-side Paree. I could not believe it, but I tell you I vill bring zo many magnums back to sweet Paree and besides, mes amis, the empty bottle makes such a good lamp.' That's the juxtaposition to pay attention to. That's the incongruity to feast on."

"Yeah, sure," she might have answered. Those soft beak lips gobbling up the brittle Fall space between them. The sense of her presence despite her absence—a disturbing, joy-wrenching sensa-tion, Moran thought and not to be cultivated.

"A phony cultivation," Moran's wife said at dinner, "and a te-dious, tedious seminar. He speaks in such a phony arch, cultivated way."

Moran smiled still on 117, still sampling chill ponds, feeling himself a mouse tucked perfectly into a vinyl black bucket seat.

"Heian marriage patterns—what do you think of them Mrs. Moran?" she parodied her professor's pronunciation. "Oh, call me . . . call me—that's what I couldn't decide—it was incredible, I couldn't decide and so there was a rather ghastly pause which had, surprisingly, the effect of making him listen. For the first time. I thought about saying—Natalie or Ms. Moran or maybe my maiden name. That seemed, at least momentarily, the very best thing to offer. I could have said something my professional career, reasserting my identity, and for purposes of creative professional-ism. It would be important for me to separate my various entities and to push forward the original me to burst through the con-structions of American marriage patterns, let alone Heian ones."

"But you said Natalie."

"Right. Call me Natalie, please. I couldn't believe my own voice—such enormous sniveling. A worm. A worm. Call me Natalie, please. Why did I add the please—didn't that seem, seem unsure of myself? Of course it did and what's more he knew it. The whole seminar knew it. It was like opening a giant walnut and shouting, 'Here's my schizophrenia, dig it!'"

The chill water in Moran's throat was warming to the soft temperature of two dark lamp shades in their small living room. The chrome sea blended away into the white plastic parson's table in front of the faded blue couch on the imitation Hopi, wool (hand woven) rug.

"What did you say about Heian marriage patterns?"

"I didn't. Harris-san interrupted me, a gesture I'm sure—he said so later—he considered a rescue operation. The maiden floundering on the seminar table like some half-dead mackerel, flopping around while Professor Cowl meditated on the coup de grace."

"Well, what did Harris-san say?"

"Some incredible appropriate spiel—actually fairly perceptive—on the constrictions of the Heian court. Women truly were oppressed, who could deny it? Nothing to do all day but flick fans and wait for Prince Genji to tire of whomever he was screwing and stop off for the night. Genji's wife, Aoi, literally went mad watching his antics. Cowl tried to maintain that since Aoi came from the lower classes she had achieved a trade-off or sorts. Status for infidelity and a shattered persona. You can see where his head is. Harris-san objected."

"You sputtered."

She looked at Moran—a silence as thick as the eleventh minute of one of his exams.

"You think that's what I did," she said.

"Not really."

"Then why did you say it?"

"To make a joke, I guess."

"That's your idea of a joke, to belittle someone."

"No! To seize on the incongruity and manufacture it. You're incredibly articulate, so I suggested you sputtered. See?"

"All too well. The fact of the matter is I had plenty to say, but Cowl kept cutting me off. 'Yes, yes, Natalie, but we really can't reverse project present dilemmas on to past societies, can we?'"

"What else is history but that?"

She paused again, "I should have told him that—that would have knocked the skinny swine cold. You're good." She leaned across the barn door they used for a dining table, kissed in a soft unbeak-like way.

They always did the dishes together. Her master's program and his employment balanced out, the remaining housework, hence to be divided.

"Harris-san pointed out, and its true enough, that Heian courtship rests on the partially seen, the deflected gesture, the sartorial hint of romance. It's actually rather incredible; how exciting can the quick swish of a sleeve behind a screen be? Apparently overwhelming. Genji responds in a fetishist way—a lacquered heel, a slow closing fan drives him up the wall, setting off a barrage of exchanged poems and presumably consummation. But all the while you get the feeling that nothing will measure up to that moment of watching the sleeve flit behind the screen. Glimpses are everything."

To wash the dishes she wore yellow rubber gloves, and for a moment they reminded Moran of the dropped board gate to shut off the commuter train at the Lincoln station.

"Love is anticipation, isn't it?" Moran said.

"Sex maybe is," she answered, "at least Harris-san thinks so."

Two weeks of commuting went by before Moran had his next opportunity. She was waiting just beyond the station and looking frantic. Moran opened the door. "Another biology test?" he called out, leaning onto the passenger seat.

She scrambled in, "Thanks. I was hoping I hadn't missed you."

"Really?"

"Oh yes, it's so hard getting a ride in the mornings. The traffic's going the other way. Yeah, another test."

"Sounds like the place is less flexible?" More said, accelerating back onto 117.

"Maybe," she answered opening her large blue notebook.

The same jeans, same sneakers, same oval face, same vulnerable presence.

"I neglected to tell you, I'm writing a biography—"

"Enh?" she turned pages without looking up.

Moran went on, "Though I don't suppose you've ever heard of him, our Ambassador to China during World War II, Clarence Gauss."

She looked at him, put her hands on the notebook.

Moran thought, she might actually have heard of Gauss. Then she lifted her hands, and looked back down at the notebook, evidently memorizing for the test.

"Gauss is rather important mostly as a kind of emblem of how our China policy would be formulated." She was alternately lifting and clamping her hands on the notebook, and Moran trailed off.

"I'm sorry," she said. "What were you saying about your house?"

"Gauss, Clarence Gauss," Moran answered, but she had gone back to the notebook. Her jeans looked dirtier and Moran watched the entirely leafless trees. He had to remind her of her stop. She thanked him and went off running clutching her notebooks like a mirror to her breast.

"Gauss was not even called to the celebrated hearings when General Hurley accused the Far Eastern Desk of State of being pro-Communist," Moran explained in lecture. "Instead he sulked in New Mexico, asthmatic as ever but issued no statements to the press. Lonely Clarence," Moran was amused to hear himself say, "Rejected of men, a man of sorrows and afflicted with grief." The undergraduate heads began to come up. Moran sent them down again with nine improvised points of Hurley's attack, nine itemized charges which if Hurley had not really made them, Moran felt in the heat of embarrassment he should have.

In the Cambridge bedroom Natalie said, "I should have gone to the lab tonight. Harris-san is always accusing me of goofing off too much."

Moran was reading, as he always did before going to sleep, a volume of Foreign Relations of the United States. There were two large windows on his left overlooking the street. Two dirty white shades, yanked down, blocked the view although glow from the street lamps came through after he had put the light out.

"You could have read as long as you like," she said.

"The China volumes just don't have their old narrative pull."

"I'm sorry."

"I bet." Moran watched as the shades began to glow like giant upended 3 x 5 cards on the wall. The ceilings were higher than any rooms they had shared and for the first time they had real carpeting (with padding) in the bedroom, but there was something hot, oppressive in the room. After a while Moran got up and opened the window nearest him. Soot came off on his fingertips. Street sounds became clearer. By the building's entrance a parked car started up.

"Can't you sleep?"

"No."

"I'm sorry. Why don't you read some more."

"I thought we might try something more active."

He waited an enormous length of time—then sat on the edge of the bed. Too much sitting in the same spot he reckoned would send them all spilling off the side. Old sloped beds, worn over, too often sat upon. Did Gauss sit up under the eaves and wonder where the action had gone? Surely there must have been a time when he saw too clearly the young language technicians were dialoguing with State over his shoulder, around his communiques, in spite of his cables. When did he first feel extraneous? Is that what sent him to the attic?

"Well?" Moran said lying back on his pillow, legs still half over the edge.

"That's about the most unflattering invitation imaginable," she started softly but the rage, dim enough at the start, was familiar. "It's as if, frankly, I haven't feelings. Only uses. Where is the style? Hell, if not the style—forget the style. What about the simple care? Forget the style. I shouldn't have brought it up."

"You didn't forget it, though did you? It's what you thought about first."

"What about care or rudeness? Jesus! The rudeness of it."

Was she sitting up? Moran brought his legs up on the bed. He expected a tirade, waited for it. Better than the China volume and something in place of something else at least—at least something to fight the heat of the room. But she turned on her side. "I'm sorry," she said again with the same intonation as the previous "I'm sorry's."

"You're sorry that I'm rude?" he countered.

She sighed, "Sorry that I don't feel like it. You really can turn me off sometimes."

"Would it be better if I dropped poems in your tea, flounced around in a blue silk kimono—spent a night in the closet licking your shoes—munching on lacquer, chewing up the very heels?"

"That might be better for you," she answered swiveling back toward him.

"Then style is all?"

"Prince Genji thought so."

He moved to kiss her and she responded only enough to indicate nothing had changed. At last a cold edge of air moved beside the bed, then slowly over it. What would be your best style, Moran thought? Beak-like lips and sneakers, oval face and clear, mesmerizing eyes? In full sway-run arms locked on books down gravel expanses to Lincoln-Sudbury High? Yes indeed, there was style enough for a thousand slow-closing fans. Prince Genji would have plastered those soft-clicking lockers with poems. Moran had trouble with a single good night kiss.

In the morning she explained over their usual toasted English muffins and single soft boiled eggs that the whole language class was spending the day at the Tufts language labs. She would be home after dinner.

"The whole day?"

"Yes."

"And dinner too?"

"Right. At a Japanese restaurant in Medford."

"The whole class?"

"Well, most of it. Swan-san, Harris-san Oda sensei, the ones who are, as Tanaka sensei says, 'are doing well.'"

Doing well, Moran thought. The phrase lingered and Moran was delighted he got a chance to use it again that morning. Once he got past the Lincoln station, he drove slowly until he found her.

"Not another test today," she said scrambling into the Datsun.

"Then you're doing well," Moran said, lingering over the pronunciation.

"Doing well?" she answered thoughtfully. "No. I'm not doing well—barely getting through, to tell the truth."

Moran thought about saying, "Me too," but said instead, "You're wearing a dress."

"I have to be in an assembly."

"A good excuse."

She laughed, arranged her books on her knees. Her legs were shaved, gorgeous, milk ivory against his black carpeting.

Doubtless pliant smooth in a way they were not yesterday and could not be tomorrow. Moran breathed slowly, turning to watch the mud brown pond.

"What's the assembly about?"

"Athletic awards."

"You're a cheerleader then?"

"Gosh no! I'm assistant manager of the field hockey team."

"I see."

"But I have to sit on the stage anyway."

They rode for a few more minutes. Moran rubbed his lower lip, then said, "Did you miss the bus for me?" Was his tone jaunty enough?

"No, really." She answered immediately, guilelessly. "I took too long dressing."

"Well, you look very good."

"Yeah, sure, dynamite. Thanks. Thanks."

There was real gratitude in the second "Thanks."

When they got to the gravel entrance of Lincoln-Sudbury High, Moran pulled off and said, "Are you worried about appearing on stage?"

"Frankly, yes," she turned toward the door.

"Well you look very good. You have nothing to worry about."

"Thanks." She started to open the door. A looming orange bus swerved around them.

"Let me tell you something—"

She looked back at him. Was there panic behind her puzzlement?

"Let me tell you something," Moran said trying to think of something to say. He thought about begging her to ride all the way to Worcester with him. Rejected it. Thought about offering her a cigarette. He didn't have any. "Let me tell you this," he said. "You look wonderful. Really good, really great and so don't you worry about, about any Harris-san-monts." He smiled.

"Any what?" she said, getting out.

"Harris-san-monts. It's a phony French way of saying harassments."

"Okay," she said stepping back, turning, hurrying down the gravel – ivory flashes like sun chips off the water darting toward the school.

Moran waited for another orange bus to come around him. Prince Genji would have done better, Moran thought. Probably done better, but he was right about the emphasis on glimpses. Moran eased the Datsun back onto 117. Genji would have been more careful, rehearsed his statements, leveled his poems so they could slip easily through the most plastic locker vent. And he would have had the time, the commitment. Genji would have done better, but he would not, could not, have written two full drafts of a biography of Clarence Gauss. That, Moran delightedly recognized, was the difference.

The Riches of This World, Part I

(Liv Wells' Imprimatur & Moran's Collapse)

"Jesus, Natalie, you couldn't wait a crummy half a day so I could get through this luncheon. Do you get it? Liv gives his final okay on the manuscript. I'm not asking for the fucking moon, only for a crummy half day."

"Isn't this our standard interaction? Your dismissal of me in the name of your imagined vision; a career moment of stupendous significance? I mean really cosmic significance, your chance to scratch the very surface of the firmament, to chrome emblazon the all-consuming gleam of your peerless reputation. Well, fuck it, and fuck you. When you come back I'll be gone. I'm done talking through our differences. I'm done imploring you for change and then listening endlessly to your promises of modification, growth, real love. Ah, real love, genuine commitment, easy empathy— things you don't have the faintest fucking idea about. Incapable. Beyond your self-absorbed, self-satisfied, self-obsessed shit–self."

"I'm getting tired of your well-rehearsed tirades. Get a new shtick."

"Fuck you! And fuck off!"

"Just a crummy half a day. We can hash this out after I get back, can't we?"

"I don't think so. I'm all done living on your time frame. You can hash things out as you say with whomever you find here."

"Does that mean you might still be here?"

"Suit yourself with whatever little Japanese wife you can find. Someone who doesn't find your actions hurtful."

He recognized her suddenly notched-down tone. Outrage instantly swallowed whole and kept at the ready in some easily-opened cage deep inside her. As if granting breathing space to him so that she might find more swiftly his most vulnerable surface. And surface was all that she apparently cared to scar. So he thought, at least momentarily, that salvage was possible. He might get a half day before the terrible reckoning he imagined was the only logical outcome of their increasingly sour hand holding.

"That's what you never seem to get: how much you hurt me. And why? Because you define what's hurtful, and dismiss whatever you deem non-hurtful. But you, asshole, don't get to define what's hurtful. You simply don't get that. I choose not to wallow in it longer. So I've solved a number of problems with leaving, and you won't have your favorite impediment around when you get back from licking whatever ass needs licking to advance your wondrous career."

He thought so this is it, at long last. Of course it would come at what he imagined was the most crucial moment. Still when he watched the kind of huffy stiffness to her apparently straightened shoulders he felt a shuddering lust to grab and slobber on her delicious neck. At her most savage dismissals, endings, cursings, he found her most ravishing. Most haunting deliciousness. If he could only throttle her, gobble her up, lick and chew on her softest most swallowable armpits, thighs, and, good God, the softest slopes of her endless stomach streaming down like the Appian Way into the softest breezeway toward Rome's glistening, wet Spanish Fountains.

It was with that tenuous, dizzying imagined consummation that he sat down at the little round table one hundred and twenty seven feet from the 18th green of Wee Burn's golf course where C. Livingston Wells was already seated with the nifty maroon box of the 656 page manuscript at his feet. The box seemed a jewel on the grey and brown flagments, the perfect dead lamb offering, Moran thought, as distraction from near ejaculatory sentiments flooding through him.

"I'm sorry to be late. Marital issues, what else is new . . ."

Wells smiled avuncularly and offered a story that turned away from what might have been an embarrassing revelation. "You know my son had a bass instructor at Juilliard, an older fellow who had standard phrase covering any late entry or any dismissive gesture toward any student he was hurrying away from. . . The old duffer said, 'So sorry, bowel disorder.' It was, I must admire, a perfect stopper. Perhaps you could try it next time."

"I'll give it due consideration," Moran said, relieved to get beyond discussing Natalie's declaration.

"Do a bit more than just sit on it," Wells said and Moran understood the opprobrium in his tone. The former Under Secretary did not like to be kept waiting. "I took the liberty of ordering us both a Prosecco, since I do believe, we've got something to celebrate, don't we?"

"You're in control of that," Moran answered.

"No, David, you've got the control. A really admirable control. I found your work really exhilarating, substantive, convincing, and I whole heartedly agree that I should have been made Secretary. That chalice passed from my lips for the most arbitrary and surprising reasons. And that was regrettable for me, of course, but more so for the country. I could have kept the whole mid-east effort in clearer perspective, if I say so myself."

"As indeed I said so, and I do believe it." Moran said.

"You did indeed. So here's to us in settling the mists of history, at least to our liking." Wells held up his flute of Prosecco and Moran dutifully followed through to clinking. "Well done, David. Really well done!"

"I hear a snippet of objection in your praise. Am I mistaken?"

"Oh, maybe some of the personal stuff. I'd abjure the public's delight in smut, in innuendo, gossip, and furtive allegations, always veneered with faux sadness about the telling. There's no Constitutional amendment concerning the right to know. The Japanese always superbly understood that. Knowledge is always, and only, in the hands of those who need to know, don't you agree?"

"That's certainly the way the Japanese handle it—still one of the toughest places on the planet to get on line." Moran said.

"I didn't notice that in any of the hotels I've stayed at." Wells poured himself a bit more Prosecco.

"The best places are exempt. Anything four or five stars," Moran said quietly.

"Not true. I used to stay in some low *ryokan* just to keep my language up."

"I don't think they ever settled you in a run of the mill *ryokan*."

"Touché," Wells said. "How's about a starter?"

"I could go for a shrimp or two."

"Splendid! I'll try the soup." Wells held up his right arm, the sleeve slipping down enough to reveal a monogramed cuff link, gold in the mid-day sunlight still chilly enough for late April in Connecticut. A young waiter in a crisp white shirt and black trousers immediately appeared. "Ah, Sebastian, we'll have a shrimp and whatever the soup is today."

"One soup or two, Mr. Wells?"

"Just one, and rather quickly if you don't mind. We're on a tight schedule, aren't we?" Wells nodded toward Moran. When the waiter left, Wells said, "I come down often enough from Yale that most of the younger staff know me. Bill got me on a so called extended membership, courtesy of the Buckley account. Bill always knew how to take care of fellows of like mind."

"I guess he never thought of you as a crypto-Nazi fascist faggot." Moran said.

"Never did, as much as I admired old Vidal." Wells laughed.

"I thought Gore's statement: 'Whenever I hear of a friend succeeding, something inside of me dies,' was the best summation of academic life ever made." Moran said.

"Well, I suppose with this," Wells gestured toward the maroon box on the flagments, "you'll have a lot of friends with dead somethings."

"We can hope. Does that mean you're on board with typesetting?"

"You've made the changes I've requested. I especially liked the way this draft moved past all that mung about conspiracy and old George Atcheson. May he rest in peace."

Moran, trying not to fix on the phrase, 'this draft' so suggestive of yet more drafts, said, "Tom Cole already did the heavy lifting on that issue."

"So he did, and rather better than I imagined him doing. He's a plodder, capable but without a shred of irony. Anyway, the Atcheson story is put to bed."

"If not the 731 issue."

"As far as I'm concerned that can come to light as fully as necessary. Our Japanese friends need reminders very regularly that they aren't special people. Aren't unique people."

"Not exceptional, like us." Moran said, watching Wells smile but not assent.

"I like your quickness, David. What's the problem with Natalie?"

Moran felt a jolt of chastisement in the question but the gentle tone with which Wells asked opened a response Moran could not apparently stop. "I think our marriage is going bung."

"Most marriages do. I'm on my third and it's hardly a sure thing."

"It's not natural," Moran said conscious of his interior structure dismantling. "It's not what I imagined. Not what I thought was happening or would happen. It's not . . . " Moran felt himself sliding toward sobbing, a bewildering experience, but, blessedly, Sebastian arrived with shrimp and soup.

"Thank you, Sebastian. Do you graduate this year?" Wells said smoothly.

"Yes sir, in a month."

"And then what?"

"I'm not sure. Maybe I'll hang around here, work here. I don't know."

"My advice, young fellow, would be to enjoy no commitments. Take your time. Sample the world. Let a year, maybe eighteen months, float where they will. Look around before you jump in. If you do that, you'll end up like this splendid fellow here, Dr. David Moran, who's writing, indeed has written, a 500 plus page biography of me. I once took time off when I was your age, and here I am, with a skilled historian writing my relation to the world. Think of that."

"Gee," Sebastian said with, Moran reckoned, a sly, slight mockery Wells might recognize but not immediately.

"I'll try the baked haddock," Wells continued, perhaps realizing the "Gee" was slightly tainted.

"Same here," Moran said, relieved to have the decision made.

As Sebastian went away Wells said, "They need some bracing, don't they. I've come to understand we all need bracing at certain mileposts. So let me offer you some, David, if that would help."

"I'm really open to it, believe me."

"Of course you are. Doubtless it seems your nicely constructed view of yourself and your world is threatened. Does little good to know such threatening will force you to grow, learn, really enlarge." Wells spread his hands apart on the beige table cloth. "But it surely will. Surprising unsteadiness will open up your sponge for life, although that's a shabby metaphor."

"I feel like a shabby metaphor." And Moran summoned Natalie looking at him over a rack of drying dishes and saying, "Jesus, let's get a new sponge—you'll find it easier than actually cleaning the sink, since you never, ever, clean the sink." And he realized he liked her verbal assaults. They validated him in a way that felt very reassuring. Just as he knew once more that he wasn't much of a person, just a construction of frail ambitions, there she was affirming his vileness. She actually thought he had substance as a target of wrath. Masochism apparently had some tenuous glow or at least pushed back handfuls of darkness. *How sorry you feel for yourself,* she said, *what sentimental dreck.*

Wells was talking again, saying something about mileposts and new beginnings, about the liberation of closure, but Moran only saw Natalie squeezing the sponge, remarking on its filth, on its inadequacy, its immediate replace-ability. She'll be gone, he thought, actually gone. When I get back she won't be there. What will that be like?

Wells was speaking louder now, "Maybe we need to get beyond life aphorisms. Not a bad idea. You want to know whether I'll put my imprimatur on the manuscript and you can proceed to that shining place on the academic hill. Isn't that so?"

Moran nodded breathing harder stifling something like a sigh.

"I could demand more drafts. I don't think you've quite grasped what a schemer Byrnes was, a very skilled infighter, and there are nuances about my take on Vietnam that you simply slide over. I'm not un-self-aware. I do wish you had put in somewhere what Gorbachev said about me. But in total here is a masterful exposition that leaves me looking pretty good, it seems to me, so I asked myself, why should I be making additional demands and in fact perhaps eliciting a less flattering picture eventually from your efforts? No one ever gets the enshrinement they believe about themselves. One should be satisfied with a reasonably positive depiction. So, yes, as far as I'm concerned; let's go forward to typesetting. Congratulations on a superbly written, near comprehensive account of my life. And I am thankful you left the business about Marlene out of this draft. This final draft."

Moran said through his unbalance and widening sense of grief, "It's no hatchet job."

"You're right, David. Actually, I can't conceive of you writing a hatchet job about anyone."

The haddock arrived in surprising sparkling foil packets. Wells unfolded his eagerly and said, "The very best way to cook fish. Keeps the flesh really moist. Be sure to squeeze the lime."

When he got home, Natalie had indeed gone. Walking in he could tell the house had a different weight, a different hollowness, a different smelling fragility. Get used to the new emptiness, Moran thought. But all that seemed premature. Of course she'd come back. Of course any new direction would be a disappointment. He was heartened to find most of her bureau drawers about half full. She'd have to come back for her things, and at the same time he knew she'd be furious that he had looked into her remaining clothing. That anger might have been all that was left of their mutual attraction. *Ultimately you're just a pile of self-pity—romantic suffering unconnected to any other person,* she'd told him often enough. *You have no idea how to live or even if you're actually alive. Tirelessly erasing every glimmer of actual care. You can't see anyone because you're constantly looking backwards over your shoulder to make sure your ass is available for licking. That's the extent you let anyone in, only for licking your ass. Otherwise no one can exist outside your guard-all shield. So what, Davy, does the future hold?*

Boundless loneliness, infinite separation from care? Oh, it might be some other avenues turn up—worldly success, available ASEAN women not be afraid of exploitation—Anyone willing, so very willing, to pretend with you. Come in little guard-all shielded world. Come within the capsule. It only costs your humanity.

-§-

B interrupted, "Aren't things slipping into each other here? Archer's world sliding into Moran's? Isn't one banishment enough?"

"Maybe," C answered "things always bleed into each other."

"Only in your silly head," B said. "Message overtakes narrative and we are all left bloated and disappointed, as if Serena began serving American style portions. Is that it? More importantly why should we give a shit about any of these people?"

"I give up," C said. "Some people admired Moran. He was a gifted lecturer/writer and the biography of Wells sold amazingly well. He might not ever have joined Guade on Olympus, but on the lower frequencies, he managed to redefine American efforts in Asia into a more favorable light. No small feat, quite beyond your sales figures of your neo-Nazi career."

A suddenly objected, "That's a bit beyond the pale, I do believe. We all have to make our way in this vale of tears and you cannot impute past sins on present strugglers. Besides that's a side tracking of any of our concerns. We need to know how things went on for David. Was it just empty success after empty success for him or did Natalie come back? Seems she keeps coming back in your tellings. Might we presume that and hold out for a new blending of their much demarcated spirits."

"What the fuck does that mean?" B asked.

"I mean," A said, "does she come back and rescue David from his aridity? Can we hold out that modest hope?"

"You can and she does. Long enough, together enough to have a child, a daughter."

"That's really great, because we don't have to wade through your lugubrious telling to get there. So what happens then?"

"Natalie leaves him permanently, taking little daughter whose name might be some C word, I haven't decided yet."

"Jesus," B said. "A C word daughter. Is that how it goes? I know the Japanese often try out a name on a child before they choose. Is that what you're up to?"

"It just means she hasn't claimed her name yet," C said. "It will have to be a strong name since her very life held things together for Natalie and David, at least for a time. And then Moran's professorial gifts sends him back again and again to Japan, eventually to governmental work as well as business connections, but always alone always tirelessly guarding his separateness so that at the very end he returns to America since he knows in exiting he belongs, as we all might know in the shrine to non-belonging that's America.. I've seen the preparation for the end, but not the end itself. I'll fill those segments in I think somehow, but try this near ending for now."

VI: A, B, C, Endings

The Riches of This World, Part J

(Last Gasp)

THE CUMULATIVE RUMBLING OF the box fan in the master bedroom usually awakened him at 3:10 a.m., or so the iridescent blue numbers of the old G.E. radio/clock indicated. And in the throb of that fan his memory coursed again over his wife's calm explanation at the end: *It's just like child birth. You remember I was very anxious, but once I found someone who could explain each step of the process, I just relaxed and everything went swimmingly. I only needed a particularly experienced mentor, a caring guide to figure out how to shed you, like a mangled foetus. That's what you are, you know—a very mangled foetus, destined I can now see never to grow into a human being. You'll have lots of the trappings, but inside nothing but mangled narcissism. So I was shown the steps, from separation, to established identity, one's own accounts, and then zipping through the nasty legalities. And presto! Autonomy! Liberation and freedom!* And it was just as she said, he thought from the middle of their queen size bed. He rested on the ridge that had separated them, hoping to wear it down so the mattress over time would be perfectly flat again. It was uncanny how much more she had known about everything. How skillfully, how evenly, she understood marital endgame.

In the morning he went downstairs, fed the cats, retrieved the morning paper from the newly painted front porch, and over a cup of Irish Breakfast tea, re-read the delicately inked letter from Korea: "It is truly remarkable that Mr. Kim said he knew you. He said you shared *kimchi* with him right after the war and wanted you to know he remembered you. Please visit him if you ever come back to Pusan. He saw your picture in Asia Marketing News" A note obviously written by someone else. It was hardly likely Mr. Kim knew any English---perhaps by his dutiful wife, if had one.

She signed the note, "Adele." Not likely a Korean, but he did remember in the barracks tent there was discussion of a Korean hooker who was designated "Adele," by the 18th year old troops who visited her just before the truce in mid-summer, 1953. And he remembered Mr. Kim, the pugnacious guard at that jail in Pusan who had knocked him down and kicked him twice in the stomach, flooding the dirt floor with the near pint of *soju* he'd drunk. And when he got his head up out of the vomit, Mr. Kim's baton splattered his front teeth back into his mouth. And yet no sooner had the fresh blood taste driven out the puke scent, Mr. Kim's baton was cradled under his chin and yanked back so that he instantly rose to his knees and then to his feet in blind, blinking desperation to save his larynx. Mr. Kim spun him around and then in a smiling moment head butted him in the nose. Next, he rammed the end of the baton into his sternum, dumping him down again in the dirt. In the next three hours he swallowed teeth, blood and vomit while his amazed buddies mopped him with their torn T shirts.

-§-

B said, "I don't get it. You seem to be mixing up Archer with Moran. Did they both have experience in Korea, during the war? That can't be. The correct ages don't add up. You've fucked something up."

"They both could have such experiences."

"Yeah, especially if time doesn't count, chronology doesn't count. Give it up."

"If they both had such experiences it's because I wanted them to. Surely that's my prerogative."

"Okay, but you're gonna lose your readers. People will figure you don't know what you're doing."

"And that worries you?"

"It ought to worry you and your publisher."

"I can regulate their worry, and yours too. Let's worry together about Mr. Kim's fate."

-§-

To rid himself of her, he would have to kill Mr. Kim—surely a chivalrous gesture she'd reject, perhaps because it came directly out of his anger at her.

Her last months were spent analyzing the eleven years of their marriage. Something he said, or some look he gave her, triggered a standard recitation: *I could never have stayed with you. I didn't understand then that I never existed for you. No, you made me a figment of your imagination, and if I didn't conform to that image you tirelessly erased me. Why did you do that? Why couldn't you actually see me? You need to examine that. If you don't, you won't ever have actually lived.*

When Mr. Kim came back he carried a large ceramic jug filled, it was immediately apparent, with fermented cabbage and pounds of garlic, as well as pulverized dried red peppers. He set the jug on the dirt floor. Then, with his baton he smashed the side of the jug so that the *kimchi* spread with wondrous odor in a widening circle of slush dirt. "You meal!" he shouted in near perfectly rehearsed English pronunciation.

The letter's innocent itemization: "you shared *kimchi* with him," wasn't exactly accurate. Perhaps it existed only in Mr. Kim's memory. Or was Mr. Kim a comedian with a big-nosed interpreter note-writer reliving his jokes? Amanuensis Adele. The record should be set straight. The promise actually fulfilled.

He would fly to Pusan, find a small ceramic jug and fill it with *kimchi*, carry it into Mr. Kim,

smash it in front of him, shout "our meal!" and then kill him by cutting his throat. Or maybe by driving four fingers into his larynx. It would be simpler and more effective to use a knife. He remembered reading that the Buddha answered his imploring disciples, that yes, he could teach them how to walk on water, but it would take years, and wouldn't it be easier to take a boat? A knife was made for cutting and not erasure.

2.

When the front stabilized at the DMZ and his tour was nearly up he'd been sent down to Pusan to oversee bodies for shipment back to the states. Pusan was the jumping off point back to the world--for the inert and the lithe alike. Each day he slowly, lovingly loaded white plastic body bags into grey painted pine coffins. Each night he wandered around the entertainment district of the city, near the docks where he worked, sampling one small bar after another, more and more deeply attached to the cylinders of strong *sochu* considered the emblem of male maturity, more and more mesmerized by the Korean phonetic characters of the menus he couldn't initially read, but soon enough could sound out perfectly and so become a welcome foreign mascot at a number of small, almost family ventures living off the G.I.s--the living "Joe" who had come to save them from Kim Jung Il's marauding minions. He liked the mud streets and thatched huts that juxtaposed cement apartment houses, and hasty hangars tossed up by the Americans in anti-Communist frenzy. Most of all he liked the dizzyingly open possibilities of war-time.

Everything needs to be open-option with you, she said. *All I can count on is your commitment to whim. Never a joint venture or true planning--always preserving the option to change everything in a trice. Why? Let me elaborate: because fundamentally you have no empathy. You are the supreme solipsist, narcissistic to the end. Oh, let me correct that. You can feel empathy so long as it meshes perfectly with your own feelings. But if there is exact duplication, why, then, the care and concern is near epic. But the slightest deviation and what ensues, let me tell you, you slimy bastard, is erasure!*

3.

Aboard the KAL flight to Seoul he couldn't resist perversity. He asked the lithe stewardess: "Is KAL still slicing into Russian air space to save jet fuel?"

But her confused response, smiling, of course, faded into the fan rumble of the jet engines roaring over Sakhalin Island. Sakhalin Island or the middle ridge of the Simmons Beauty Rest Queen size mattress. "Are you hungry?" the stewardess answered.

"No, but I need help reserving a train down to Pusan."

"There are many flights," she answered. "The airport is not near the station. I could get you a flight."

"I prefer the train. I want to see the country up close, but not too close."

Intimacy was always your bugaboo, she said often enough, *you function well enough with anyone at a distance, and kept at a distance, but we inhabit this tiny space (like the first class section) day in day out, and we keep each other company, don't we? But you only keep company with your weird projection of me, not me. And shortly you will have spent all this time with me and not known me. Doesn't that make you sad? Worse yet, you won't have known yourself. Surely, that has to bother you. Apart from your projection of me I might be a person you could actually love, not the apparition of your endless, thoughtless, unquestioned conjuring. Wouldn't you like to find that person, love that person?*

Oh yes, he thought, these trains don't equal those in Japan. Not as smooth, not as soundless and never quite matching the numbers on the side of the cars with the numbers on the platform–unthinkable in Japan. And still filled with cigarette smoke. On the other hand there were more hills to slice through, more rivers to cross, and a much more impatient and vocal clientele. People actually argued here. All those quiescent years in Japan and here couples barked at each other as if life could be no other way.

He was reassured only when he saw a Daimaru Department store in downtown Pusan. For years he'd shopped Daimaru in Osaka. There was wonderful predictability--groceries in the cellar floor, bargain ceramic dishes on the top floor. Narrow escalators linking everything. On the third floor, in kitchen equipment, he found the best knife for killing Mr. Kim.

"Ceramic edge. Never dull," the clerk, a short stocky woman perhaps twenty-five or so years old and wearing some kind of orange apron, said with marvelous English diction. So much better than what he'd heard in Japan.

"I need it to gut a human being," he said, smiling.

She seemed to absorb the words and responded, "Good for ducks."

"I need it to cut a man's throat," he said again, confident she didn't grasp what he meant.

"It's very sharp and stain-proof," she answered.

"He's a very old man and I bet his throat is very tough."

Although he was certain she didn't follow what he was saying, he none the less was startled when from her apron she produced a shining piece of nylon rope, flipped it on a nearby cutting board and with three swift strokes severed the squealing strands into two pieces. He wondered if the knife could cut the coils along the Beauty Rest ridge.

He slowly ascended to the top floor and threaded his way between aisles holding bins of tiny dishes like so many ceramic giant seagull droppings. He passed the rice bowls, passed the handless tea cups, to the "English tea section" and stopped among sugar bowls with tops. He needed something very small and cylindrical, suggestive of the huge pepper urn/vases that he remembered on the balconies of every Pusan apartment in 1953. Something so emblematic as to summon memories of violence and vomit. But the English bowls were too squat, and eventually he had to settle for a very small sugar bowl that at least was the requisite deep brown color. The sides were fragile enough that he was fairly certain a swift flail of the knife's thick handle would splinter the dish, and the *kimchi* purchased in the grocery section would flow out before Mr. Kim's astonished eyes. In the grocery section he delighted in asking for 200 grams of *kimchi* using Japanese, said slowly, as if to compensate for imagined ignorance-- *ni haku gramu, kudasai.* But the clerk behind the counter casually tossed one tiny scoop into a plastic bag, weighed, labeled and handed it back, saying , "What else?"

4.

At St. Paul's Silver Housing Complex, Mr. Kim was confined to a wheelchair. There was a bar across his lap, and periodically he strained rising against the bar, as if to stand up out of the chair.

The nurse said, "He wants to move around, but sometimes he's too violent."

"I can believe that. I've experienced that a long time ago. Are you Adele?"

"No."

It seemed he was destined never to know Adele in his life. So best to get on with it.

"I've brought some *kimchi* to share with Mr. Kim. Maybe it will stir his memory."

"Kimchi is very usual here."

"I understand that, but I'd like to share it with him privately. Back in his room."

Without comment she steered the chair down two halls and into a tiny room with grey linoleum on the floor, gray painted walls, and a window with swirls of brown dirt smeared across it. He could see the grassless field of an elementary school through the dirty window.

"Please feel free to leave. We'll be fine. If there's a problem I'll come and get you."

She didn't respond immediately and seemed to be checking his expression about to comment, as his wife often did, that he'd gone glossy, distancing himself from whatever they were discussing--invariably her challenges to his attitude or behavior. "I will be nearby," she said leaving the room.

He pulled up a metal chair and seated himself directly in front of Mr. Kim. Then he lifted up the narrow, blond Formica-topped tray attached to the chair, placing it on top of the restricting bar.

"Do you remember me?" he said softly, putting the squat brown *kimchi* bowl on the tray.

"I swore I'd kill you someday, if I lived through your beating, and here I am to execute that promise. Do you understand that?"

Mr. Kim didn't look up. He apparently crossed and re-crossed his hands under the tray, and slowly something like mucus dribbled out of the left side of his mouth.

"You were the toughest son of a bitch on the police force, weren't you? You loved kicking the crap out of G.I.s didn't you? So now's here one come back to cut your fucking throat." He took out the ceramic knife. And holding it by the blade he decided a backhand motion would most decisively smash the *kimchi* bowl. But he realized the breaking bowl might summon help from beyond the room. There might not be time to reposition the knife in his hand and finish Mr. Kim off. With his left hand he upended the bowl, dumping the top and the *kimchi* out on the tray. The fiery cabbage juice slowly dripped off the tray into Mr. Kim's lap. His hands rubbed the juice and he brought his fingers quickly to his mouth. At the first taste he smiled, and said "Ah," and then added. "Sank you!" His head slumped down again, and more mucus came out of his mouth, though now somewhat rose-tinged.

Of course I couldn't kill him, he said. *Of course you couldn't she answered. Passive aggressives can't act except in moments of exceptional rage. It was all so predictable. At the climax you'd move away from self-discovery. Something would distract you---blessed distraction. In another second you'd erase the whole adventure. And now there'd be no one to call you back. You'd fashion that other you: wandering among Pusan night spots, or listening to the low decibel beat of the window fan. And there'd be no one to call you back.*

Oh, call me back, he cried softly, kneading the loose sheet across the BeautyRest middle ridge.

5.

At 3:00 a.m. his daughter called. He knew even before he groggily picked up that Cora would be finishing her day teaching in Tokyo, probably waiting for the 98 bus to take her back to Meguro, and probably amused that she'd be awakening him some twelve hours behind.

"I thought we agreed to do this only on the weekends," he said before she said "*Moshi, moshi.*"

"I figured you'd be up anyway. Aren't you? Even if you weren't, it's good to break your routines and be reminded somebody cared enough to wake you up."

"I will remember that, thankful to the end."

"More morbid thoughts eh?"

"Some morbid thoughts. Yes. Some. It comes with the territory."

"That's precisely the point. Marlene and I were talking it through last night. It doesn't have to be you alone, mooning over mom's leaving. It doesn't have to be that way."

"Oh, but it does. If no one laments you, you'll never rest in peace."

"Yeah, I read that somewhere, but that's not the important thing. You're alive and Mom never imagined you'd be basket case thirty years on, still wailing the night away for your partner."

-§-

B suddenly interrupted, "Wait a minute. One minute. When you said you weren't sure who this story applied to, I went along with that old saw. But now it seems you're blending an ending for two. Moran on one side, since Natalie never could stand him, and Archer on the other who surely was transformed by Jenna. So what's going on here? You can't blend the two. They're very different ages, aren't they? Very different experiences. Very different wives. Wholly different, and don't give me that Japanese crap that different means wrong."

"But that's still the best translation for *chigao*," C said. "Since I'm telling the story, why can't I aim it wherever I want, blend whatever I like, erase whatever reality you think interferes with the telling?"

"You can do any damn thing you like, but I don't have to keep reading or listening if you strain things outside what's actually possible. And A and I don't have to keep reading and listening. Surely you understand that."

"I understand that I'm not bound by the little postures of 'reality' —whatever that means—you and A have inside your mechanisms of perception . . . "

"What the fuck does that mean?"

"It means you might need to adjust your blinders so that an ending of Moran/Archer could slip through your ever-widening sieve."

141

"A very crummy mixed metaphor. Nobody wants to go to the considerable effort of wading through your turgid prose just to learn the rules of understanding are constantly changing. I've got better things to do. So does A."

"I regret the metaphor and I cheerfully accept most people have much better things to do than sort through my prose. So let's let the story run its course. Maybe by the end a resolution will emerge that narratively you can accept."

"And if it doesn't"

"Then I'll erase you or it. But either way the action will continue." C said solemnly, "and myriad readers somewhere will accept what has gone on. So let's get back to the teller's reaction to the term, 'partner.'"

-§-

"Partner" lingered in the static sound of phones, gently lifting upward as if to sanctify something he knew was not all that special, even in the sad distortions of reminiscence, something that might require flame-thrower memory removal (he could hear her saying, "your alcoholic all-or-nothing approach"); but in Cora's case cried out for sanctification. Didn't somebody write somewhere that the six rivers of Hiroshima actually caught fire after the detonation, or did the flames emanate only from the floating bodies, not the river proper?

"Are you there?" Cora asked.

"Certainly. I was caught by your use of 'partner.' I never thought of your mother as a partner. Although, now that I think about it we surely had our law-firm moments."

"Any relationship does," Cora said easily.

"I'm not fond of 'relationship' either. Surely there wasn't any, for a long, long time." The automatic hostility of his tone surprised him. And in the static on the line he was thousands of miles away in Florida 20 years ago watching as Cora and Marlene wrestled, scratching, yanking, slugging each other. In an amazing hostile hug they fell shattering the glass coffee table incasing shells which fractured in a terrific skittering, clacking sound on

142

the cold terrazzo floor of their little bungalow, a cold that suddenly funneled through his numb feet, nearly clamping his present breathing.

He said, "I know you speak from direct experience, and I got to watch it and pick up the pieces, didn't I?"

"Anger is part of grief," Cora countered. "We still want you to come back over. We can redo the touristy things—Hakone, Miyajima, the Noto peninsula, Kyoto. Or the Namba nightscene for old times. We could visit the places we lived, when things were better."

"When things were papered over."

"Papering over sometimes is all that we have together," Cora countered again.

"Does Marlene concur?"

"She doesn't think in our patterns and that's a blessing and why we're still together."

"You're a lucky girl."

"I am indeed and you can share in it. Come over."

It was a neat trick she had learned from her mother: the quick slide over the abyss by pretending it didn't matter. All that need be attended to was the quotidian extent of immediate logistics. Heartbroken? Try to catch the 5:05 *kyuko* from Jiyugaoka station. Want to dredge betrayals from the past and savor savageries never taken back, never answered? Decide between rye and multi-grain rolls, or discuss the relative merits of Irish Breakfast versus Earl Grey tea. Sobbing with grief? Here's a sweater. At the entrance to the abyss, in the thrall of sudden recognition that incalculable emptiness has a wondrous dark falling quality to it, and despair's parachute has only thin cords climbing the wind— the canopy torn away. At that instant suddenly acknowledge that a lot of keepsakes are fake. He said, "Have you noticed that?"

"Noticed what?"

"A lot of memories are fake."

"No kidding. A lot of artistry is fake. Maybe grief is fake. Maybe not. Come over and we can sort it out."

"We?"

"The three of us. You should be used to it. Whatever else, mom is Decide now. Don't think it over. Decide right now."

6.

Decision time in Japan, he remembered, is always lengthy, but implementation is always rapid-fire, near instantaneous. Consensus takes time. In America the opposite was true. Decisions came lickety-split but implementation took forever. Simple truisms to live by or better yet, ignore, better still: dismiss. The business guides were full of cross-cultural truisms.

Decide now, echoed from Tokyo as he slumped back in the middle of the BeautyRest. He liked the way the individual coils yielded to the lumpiness of hip and knees, and in that targeted yielding he remembered lying on the unyielding deck of the ferry down from Osaka to Hiroshima. Of course she listed Miyajima first of things to re-live. The three of them uncomfortable but so enthralled beneath their common blanket, heads on green rubber pillow bricks (for a deposit of some yen amount he couldn't remember). He did remember they had learned from the other passengers, how to stand close together and wrap the blanket around all of them. Then they could with modesty shed clothing for the coming communal sleep.

Then they slumped down carefully sheltered in the scratchy wool, feeling each others' naked legs, suddenly a very close family—perhaps the only time he realized what might have been possible, but surely passed away in the ferry's quiet slicing of the placid Inland Sea. And Cora nudging him started laughing as only four year olds can, a convulsing celebration of their absurdity on the dank hard deck. An insane underwear pajama party. He wondered if Cora shared that memory with Marlene and worried that she would invest it with perversity. He knew Marlene, in escalating tones, savaged every family memory from which she by definition had been excluded. She found taint in every fond sharing, and it occurred to him on his BeautyRest that indeed every memory had a diseased tag waiting for the right neuron to pass by, as effortlessly as the ferry that night eased toward Hiroshima.

He found himself suddenly saying to Cora, through the static. "Do you remember that resort on a *Gone With The Wind* theme?"

"Scarletto?"

"Yes, that's the name I couldn't remember. Scarletto, with fake columns. Do you remember what happened there?"

He waited for an answer but one didn't come. "The owner asked you which was the most beautiful carp in the pond out front before the columns."

"Let's not relive it."

"Do you remember how heartbroken you were when the very same carp still wiggling was brought to our table cut on its sides so you could pull pieces of its very fresh flesh off?"

"Why are you bringing this up?"

"Because I just realized I'm the carp. I'm the carp. And if I come back over you and Marlene will just pull the flesh off, bit by bit by bit. I wouldn't last an hour. Oh maybe an hour but not a full day, not a week. And you wouldn't even know you're doing it. Just seeing you would do it. "

"I thought we'd gone through enough therapy to avoid the victim game, Marl and I."

"You're right, so let's avoid it altogether."

"Now you're supposed to hang up. And we end up never talking again."

"Ah, you are you're mother's daughter."

"Oh, Jesus! I really did think we'd all gone through enough therapy to get by that congruence. Marl says we feast on it. I thought she was pouring it on a bit, but I guess she wasn't."

Marlene pouring it on flashed into him suddenly in the brilliant morning Florida sunlight and the splintering glass coffee table, shards pirouetting upwards, collapsing onto the terrazzo with echoes down his gulping throat.

"Are you hanging up?"

"Hanging on."

"So come over here and we'll hang on together. Or Marl and I will chew up your carcass."

"It's enticing, but it's not going to happen."

"Well, think about it, will you?"

Did he hear relief in her voice? He often heard relief in the voice of women in his life as he promised to leave.

On his BeautyRest, coils sponging up and down, he felt his life ricocheting between soft legs beneath a scratchy blanket or shriveling, pooling-downward human beings partnered with him on that swaying slack rope over the bottomless canyon of memory colored pastel one moment, only to be followed by the next in squid ink black.

Cora's judgmental voice called him back. "Okay, Dad, we'll try again tomorrow, about the same time. Why don't you research the costs of getting over here."

Oh, I know the costs, he thought, and they're entirely too much. "Yes, I'll do that," he said with, he felt, a certain charming disengagement in his tone, a savoir such as only the truly exiting could summon.

Oh, exit now my heart, he thought, amused by the wracking self-pity it implied even now in his supremely safe BeautyRest confinement. I'm on the very crest of the ridge, flattening it, so as he slid his hand down across the cooling sheet toward the slope she had forced into the mattress, he was certain she was there, tenderly mocking his tears.

-§-

At Serena B said, "Of course, it's not Archer's story. I mean it doesn't work out as anyone would have expected Archer's story to work out. He and Jenna seemed so compatible near Kobe, at the church—a perfect little couple. Like any of us and our wives . . . God bless them all."

"You're right. It's not the way Archer should end up. I used to think they'd perish in an aftershock—say, a 5.8 while they were eating some faux sausage in *San Ban Gai*." C said.

"I'd like that," B said.

"Yes, it would fit your nature, wouldn't it?" A interrupted.

"So it's the conclusion of the Moran and Natalie story. She wouldn't have put up with him, his crummy indecision and his stupid vulnerability." B said.

"Or her snarling judgments of him," A added. "He needed a Japanese wife who doubtless felt all her hurts but buttoned them safely in a bureau in a room Moran never entered. Neither one of them would have soldiered on to final nothingness."

"Nothingness?" C said, holding his notebook page up for just an instant. "Maybe it's not just the Japanese who take up the red thread forever. Can we say that?"

"Oh, we can, but it won't get us much. Show us another ending," A said. "Something with lively, majestic joy."

"Jesus!" B added, "Let's not get carried away."

"What's left beyond being carried away? What else is there here instead of the *Yamanote-sen*?"

"The Romance car to Hakone. Some kind of *onsen* heaven—surely there must be a super-hot springs in the sky." B said.

"All right, then, let's try something upbeat and marvelous," C said loudly and produced from his cloth grocery bag yet one more manila folder.

The Riches of This World, Part K

(Archer Unspooled)

He tended to believe that for every ecstasy there was an equivalent rancor in the normal course of living. It was a salving aphorism by which he monitored his feelings moment by moment. Squirreled away somewhere (probably undiscoverable) there was a compensating mechanism that issued "wrong slips" to match every "right credit." It might take unexpected time, but ultimately compensation smoothed all irregularities. A suitable adjusting structure was solidly in the steam of things as reality's clippings moved through his consciousness—until she appeared in his frame of the world.

She made compensation irrelevant. Her appearance doubled the sun's light. The light around her blinded him and blimped him to an altitude utterly beyond his grasp. He believed to the very end no parachute, no continental-wide-open umbrella, no palm of God, could have safely landed him back to his previous existence. Yet there he was and without hunger for any sort of compensation, beyond hunger of every sort, just to be in her company.

And there was the sex and social action, even the soupcon of social justice. He was the reconstruction project and once so easily did she reconstruct him. Free of that repair scaffolding he could take up the task for others suffused with her grace. God's sudden surfeit, dizzy with the anticipation of listening to her, smelling her nearness, alive to her smiles, tears, laughter. Alive in a way he had never felt at any time in Japan. And indeed not at any time in his life. Not in family closeness, not in studied Japanese esthetics, not in school aloofness, or the delights of new knowledge.

She beckoned; he responded. They took up her tasks, her obligations, her myriad responsibilities, her storehouse of grace and graceful accomplishment. The resurrection of addicts, the education of toddlers, the distribution of sandwiches to the poor and homeless, or the addicted and disabled—actions via the muttered references to Christian ethics and, anon, Jesus.

Soon enough they left Escondido to Mission soup kitchens in Flagstaff, Stockton, and San Francisco where he reapplied for assignment from the Board of Presbyterian Missions Abroad. Archer and Jenna requested Japan, requested and with specific and helpful (he imagined) reference to his pastor father and family killed in the war.

The return churned up old anxieties and delights, suppressed meticulously translated atrocities, as well as delightfully chill *zara soba*, imaginatively recreated and worried over charred bones of sister, father, mother, balanced off by the astonishments of Tokyo Disney Land's American town with a steel roof overhead, and *cully rice-su* alternative to fried chicken. And everywhere reconstruction gleaming as if daring the Americans once again to level the place, burn it to the ground and annihilate anew his always amazed happiness. They arrived in Osaka with Jenna expecting a child, delivered in the Awaji district in an area studded with porno theaters and "turko massage parlors." They floated above them so he imagined, transcending them in a magical Buddhist/Christian conviction that seemed to thread together the addictions and snarls of his life.

The church's mission was tardily accomplished. They spent two years surviving by teaching English at various Language Laboratories and volunteering in a Namba, Osaka soup kitchen until a chaplain job turned up in a posh Senri Chuo medical facility outside of Osaka. A second child came again via Awaji's porn district at the Seventh Day Advent's Hospital. Meanwhile Archer and his family attended the Kobe Union church in Rokko, between Kobe and Osaka. And the kindly somewhat jaded rector Rev. Robert Bonneau baptized and blessed the first, the second, and a third child of theirs. The Mission gave them, always, more than adequate, occasionally Western Style, housing and gradually Archer came to believe this remarkable largesse, and his increasing, amazed joy of family life that these evident miracles were recompense for all the suffering he endlessly translated for American exploitation and use against enemies domestic and foreign. That bothered him, but the wondrous soft shield of life in Japan spread over his anxieties. He watched his children flourish in the International Schools. He watched them absorb the dizzying freedom and safety of Japan, and that watching overwhelmed his occasional tinges that everything rested upon unacknowledged atrocity. If this milieu had its dark side, surely that was miniscule compared to the wonders, gentleness, esthetic focus, communitarian commitment of its infinitely larger light side.

And the post Korean War cornucopia of Japanese economic efflorescence spewed yen everywhere. Sakura-yen indeed, bursting into crisp packets of 10,000 yen notes and falling gently to the earth of their Postal Savings Accounts, so that more and more blossoms fell from English classes available at will, or seminars about American Studies cascading out of educational agencies born overnight and filled with housewives, salarymen, after-hours students bent on overseas travel and study. And occasional lectures or speech contest judging and everywhere packets of 10,000 yen notes. Would he talk about Jesus and wine? An hour for sixty thousand, or better yet, and hour and fifteen for ninety? Plus transportation expenses and if necessary an overnight stay at whatever hotel seemed best to him? And double everything if they would take a Q and A session in Japanese. But not too much of that lest they lose their luster as breathing "native speakers of English," invaluable in building the new globally minded Japan.

And the globally minded Japan continued spewing yen in great spurts. Soon enough an addition to the house in the rural areas now reachable aboard the Toyoko-sen, and miraculous beyond belief, an automobile so that their children could attend the vaunted American School on the far west side of Tokyo. It was as if Archer was destined to duplicate the ending of the Book of Job. Having been fire-robbed of everything, family was given back to him in proportions to obliterate his survivor guilt. Japan, as always, smacked down celebration with an earthquake in Kobe, gas attack in Tokyo subway, tsunami in Sendai—stunning reminders that when God looked the mountains skipped like goats, the sea spread wings of engulfment, but miraculously nothing harmed Archer, Jenna and the children. He knew that salvation stemmed solely from the grace that spun out of her daily in a love he could not comprehend, only marvel at, run furiously toward, passionately embrace, and enviously study. "Yes, Daddy," he found himself saying almost daily, "she knows the way beyond the slosh and, alas, you're not here to let her lead you."

"Remember," his father warned him, "even the Buddha overlooked original sin. Just as you reach satiety you'll doubtless burst into fleshy chips."

But such darkness simply vanished in her light. Her puzzled evocation of love wiped doubt away. Daily Archer thought, if only I could have shown them you, what deliverance you would have provided them. And even now in the sparse comfort of The Pilgrim's Way Archer often thought he must show the grandchildren the miracle of her loving essence so that they unconsciously would know the salvation that had evaded his suddenly torched family.

-§-

C said, "That good enough for you? I could pull a few more stops out."

"Not necessary," B said. "It might be you do rage and anger better than celebration and acceptance."

"In any event," A said, "let's accept that our trough of affirmation is now sufficiently full and you can show us something from the less appealing side. Would you do that?"

"Happy to oblige."

The Riches of This World, Part L

(Waldo's End)

In the rural cemetery Waldo and LP dig a grave for Waldo at the edge of the gun club range, yet within sight of Ernie's Car Wash and what once had been a pool hall but was now a night club and after-hours bar staffed by tall women who had failed their audition for better pay at Hooters but who still carried their tray of test tubes of vodka shots in a buxom-thrusting, aggressive fashion. LP found them mesmerizing.

An unsightly improbable pair: Waldo in a dark grey pin stripe suit, LP in dirty khaki's and loose T shirt with a vast yellow rose print on the front. Both men leaning on shovels and sweating heavily.

"We have to go down below the frost line, so it means deeper and deeper." Waldo says, still panting from exertion. Dutifully, LP jumps back into the pit and begins ladling out shovelfuls of the rock-strewn grey red dirt. Watching him Waldo imagined there should be a Japanese touch to this drama. After LP kills him, he should, ala Mishima's Lieutenant, kill himself in way that guaranteed both bodies end up at the bottom of the pit. But that meant there'd be no one to fill in the hole. Drat! Bad planning, indeed. Maybe the enterprise should be abandoned. But Waldo admired LP's determination.

"Okay, widen the pit. Scrape down the sides and elongate—I mean extend, or lengthen, make it longer. That's right. Keep scraping down that end. When it's long enough I'll come down and help." Says Waldo, hoping it takes LP a good bit of time—enough to get Waldo's racing heart beat back into dull, normal range. Waldo thinks, ASEAN men are small but they tackle hard stuff with robotic intensity, and that's really enviable. And they don't need encouragement, but he can't stop himself: "Terrific work, LP, another minute and I'm right there beside you. We're almost done." And an after-thought: "We don't want it so deep we can't get back up out of it." Waldo chuckles and jumps down.

In five minutes they have the pit shaped into a neat rectangle with sharply delineated sides all around. They rest on their shovels and seem to draw nourishment from the late afternoon spring time air. Overhead Waldo notices three circling crows and smiles at how unlike they are to the condors of his imagining. The pit is deep enough such creatures if they could transform into condors, couldn't quite get at his severed body. Their wingspans would prevent it. "You know, LP, we're only about ten feet from the Jelliffe mausoleum. Do you know that term? Mausoleum, it's an above ground kind of shrine to my dead relatives. Lots of them. Most in ash containers . . . small. But lots of them, inside the mausoleum, the structure, like a little house for the dead." Two of the distant crows settled into the still leafless branches of a giant maple tree.

"I'll dig a little indentation in the side wall," he points with his toe at the location, "and then you can go up first. You use it as a toe hold. You understand 'toe hold'?"

LP stares at him and Waldo decides he understands. He kicks an indentation with his cap-toe oxford shoes, points to it and motions LP over. In the pit they have some difficulty getting by each other. LP stands staring at the sidewall and the indentation. Waldo bends down and points with his right hand to the indentation. "Step here. Put your shoe here and lunge up."

With some exasperation he tries to lift LP's right foot toward the indentation. But LP doesn't get it, so Waldo motions him aside to the other end and says, "I'll show you." Waldo fixes his right foot's toe in the indentation. "See it's leverage, and now I can throw my other leg over the edge and pull myself up." Waldo tries it and realizes he'll need another toe hold for his left shoe on the end wall. So he kicks a second indentation about halfway up the end wall. He slumps back on the pit's solid floor and then neatly executes the exit—first the right foot into the wall indentation then the left foot into the end wall and finally the right shoe swung up over the edge. Then with his hands over the edge Waldo pulls himself out of the hole. He stands up, then kneels down and extends his arms toward the indentations. LP easily duplicates the maneuver as Waldo yanks him back up onto the grass. LP stands then kneels and pulls the two shovels out by their stained handles.

Waldo examines both shovels and picks the newer one since it seems to have a slightly sharper blade. He runs his thumb and forefinger along the blade as if to both clean and sharpen it. "This is the one, all right," he says to LP. "This one will do the deed."

"Deed?" LP says.

"The act itself. The doing of it. Not the document. What you'll actually be doing. But there's no need to hurry things, is there? We have time to savor this fine late afternoon. Savor means delight in.

Do you understand?" Waldo sets the shovel down and brushes the dirt off his suit.

LP follows along, brushing the dirt from his pants. The armpits of his rose T shirt are darkened with sweat. Waldo thinks but doesn't say, No amount of brushing will remove those.

"When the time comes—moments from now—when the time comes I'll kneel down so that my shoes are over the edge. When you do the deed, when you dispatch me, the thrust of your shovel will naturally drive me into the hole," he motioned to the emptiness behind him. "Then all you have to do is pile the dirt back in on top of me. Do you understand? We've talked about this a lot. I'm sure you get it."

LP nods.

"Do you know how many Jelliffes are buried here? I think I told you, but maybe I didn't. Twenty seven. Twenty-seven. The oldest died at ninety-seven, the youngest at two. Early Jelliffes usually didn't get past two. Maybe five. Yes, if you got past your fifth birthday you lived a long time, if you were a Jelliffe. Lots of longevity. I'm sixty one. Probably twenty years older than you, don't you think? I'd probably live into my nineties, don't you think? Not that you'd think about it much, or care that much. But I suspect you'd care more than you'd let on, wouldn't that be the case? I'd like to think so."

With the sweep of his palm-up open right hand, Waldo directs LP's gaze across the cemetery. "It's impressive, isn't it? Lot of trees. Oak and Maple for sure, but some Cherry and a couple I don't know. In another month the leaves will block a lot of the sunlight. People come here in the fall just to see these trees, did you know that? Mason Jelliffe commissioned this place. Back in the days it was on the outskirts of Worcester. Outskirts are not what you think, if you think about the term, which I suspect you don't. Anyway, the place was called 'Rural Cemetery' then because it was truly rural. But now, that's ridiculous. But the name stuck. Ridiculous. You could come back in the autumn and look at the leaves when they've turned. It's a spectacular display of color. Spectacular, unless of course it's a lousy rainy fall and chilly before its time. In which case the colors will look washed out. Disappointing. Mason gets the central spot in the monument, but we're outside the fence. Not even part of the cemetery. But we've got the choice view, even it's through the fence. Choice view and maybe the Jelliffes are like an Aspen grove with every one of us from the same root spine, a single spine and fifty different trees. Maybe the Jelliffe spine will come under the fence to gather in our little pit."

Waldo turned back toward the hole and says with a deliberate softness as if he feared being overheard, "Look, LP, I'll kneel with my back to the hole. But near enough so that my shoes will actually be over the ledge. Then we'll do it as we've rehearsed. Exactly as we rehearsed. You'll use this shovel and remember to have the shovel curvature pointing down, not up, but down. And remember, you thrust it straight ahead, as if it were a spear. Straight ahead, right at my neck. Right at my beautiful Adam's Apple. You got it?"

LP nods approval.

"But we can wait a minute, take a minute. Maybe rehearse a bit? If I smoked a bit, this would be the time. A nice long cigarette beforehand. That's how it's supposed to go, right?"

LP pinches his nose and runs some extracted mucus down the back of his hand.

"Show me how you're going to do it, will you? A practice run with nobody kneeling just yet."

LP picks up the requisite shovel and somewhat lackadaisically spears it straight out about three feet from the ground.

"Good enough," Waldo says, refusing to grade the effort. "All right I'm composed now. You need to remember what happened to your family. Think about that. Think about it. This will be different. No machetes. Just a shovel. But maybe you can get them all back. I'm going to kneel down now, with my shoes out over the edge, as far over as I can without toppling in. Without falling in. Think about your family. I'm thinking about mine."

Waldo takes his kneeling position, oxford black shoes extended over the edge of the pit. "Come ahead, stand about three feet in front of me, and aim the curved edge right here," Waldo grasps his neck under his chin. "Right here, after I take my hand away. With enough force to drive my body into the pit. If you go clean through, that's okay. There will be enough momentum to send the rest of me over the edge. And my head will find the rest of me in the pit. Remember, just as we played it out before. When

I take my hand away you drive the edge of the shovel forward. You get free and I get free too. Just like we practiced."

Waldo rocks a bit to position his knees a bit more loosely in the unpacked dirt and then takes his hand away. LP drives forward. The shovel's edge cracks through Waldo's neck that somehow takes hold of the metal of the shovel wrenching it out of LP's grip, as Waldo's severed body topples back downward into the cleanly dug coffin. The shovel appears awkwardly upright in Waldo's crumpled body and LP hears a muffled hissing and gagging sound. Then silence. By lying down LP manages to grab the shovel from Waldo's throat, freeing it for final use. In forty minutes LP fills the hole with adjacent rocks and dirt piles. He re-sods the rectangle, carries the one shovel to the truck, changes to a faded blue denim shirt with two chest pockets, and then walks slowly to the bar/night club across the street. He's not so anxious to see the tall women, since in his mind's eye he again watches his mother and sister attempting to deflect machete blows.

The Riches of This World, Part M

At Serena B said, well before the starter arrived, "How am I supposed to feel about Waldo's exit? It seems like some kind of parody, as if you got tired of wrapping things up and decided to liven things with violence, i.e., stupid blunt trauma"

"Violence came naturally to LP," C said. "And maybe for Waldo too, since he really couldn't change anything in his living situation. Just rebel against it, trash it somehow by scoffing at its evident reverence for longevity and family lineage. But you're right, I did get tired of these people. So did Mme Vincouvier."

"Good God! Did she read all this stuff?"

"Yes,"

"Actually read it? All of it?"

"More than you."

A said, "That wouldn't be hard, since he's not much of a reader."

C added, "Neither is she. Both are doers in this world and revel in it. Something for which they should perhaps be punished, and will be shortly."

"What are you going to do?" B asked, "Hire some Yakuza thugs to break my and the Madame's kneecaps?"

"It's an idea."

"You don't have the *nemawashi* to handle it smoothly. You could hire me to smooth the way to my own demise." B said, chuckling.

"I don't have to hire anyone, as well you know. I can simply write you out of this story."

"You might be able to write me out, but not my commentary." B insisted.

"You forget I'm writing both."

"Here, grab a hold here. I'm real. " B insisted.

"I don't see you on the next page."

"That's ridiculous. We've been meeting for decades, and so has A."

"I'm sending you back to semi-colon status, perhaps just a comma."

"Here, smell my port-lingering breath; incidentally I'm getting quite fond of the Portuguese. Wonderful people, with wine and ceramics, and considerable naval history. Lisbon is quite hot now, attracting attention and investment. So fuck you and your crummy attempt to write us out."

"Sales records won't save you."

"The wealth of the world has moved to Asia. Here's where sales will be made. And we're right on the cusp of that unfurling." B said, hotly.

"You're no more on the cusp of my screen."

"You haven't the guts to erase me. Much less him," B pointed to A.

A said, "What he's trying to say is that we're fundamental to your work. We show what is effective and what's fatuous and will be rejected by even the sparest of readers. We're the foil you need to keep at it. Whatever identity you're working out we've prodded you along the way and incidentally endured some really stupid self-protecting detours. We've told you to summarize some and show others. You could not have made your way without our signposting."

"What you actually are, truly are just signposts, little markers amid the litter I've been collecting, so now I'm getting tired of giving you lines," C said.

"You dumb little shit. You're not erasing me. I'll put a shovel through your throat first." B said.

"Done that. And even you thought it was off target."

A said, "You cannot make a play of our lunches, of our attention to your efforts. We're inseparable, linked tighter than anything you might write."

"It won't wash. I'm getting rid of you. Family erases Lewis, Estelle erases Janice, Estelle erases Annie May, Archer erases Ginny, Waldo erases Suzan and LP, David erases Natalie, and soon enough C erases A and B. Listen carefully and you can hear their diminishing squeals of objection, their pathetic attempts to make it into typescript reality. I know you can't accept that I made all these things. I constructed them. What can you build for me? Nothing. I speak, but you don't hear, because I don't give you the syllables of expression. You're nothing to me."

"Jesus! You've really gone over the edge," B said. "You're in some narcissistic, identity dark place, and you're not such clever company anymore."

"And you're nowhere on the next page."

"Stop that sadism. We've known you most of our lives here."

"Perhaps you're right. You don't deserve erasure. How about some lingering death? I mean look at your skin. I can see lesions forming as we talk. Little blisters that need attention, even now it what appears to be an advanced state. Let's ask her for some hydrogen peroxide and gauze pads. Or worse yet let's send you to a specialist of blood disorders who tells you about the strange form of Leukemia you've contracted. And how did you contract it? From exotic women of different cultures who drive, or better, are driven in your most luxurious Tiguans? You Tiguan master, you! I can promise you'll make it to the next page, but only through your suffering, whereas A perishes in a stroke."

"A stroke? How banal! I must ask for some better termination, something more uplifting."

"Hold up your arm and let me inject some of Daisy's final medicine."

"That's a cheap memory."

"All memories are cheap refashionings of what cannot be accepted unconditionally. Or do I sound too portentous now?" C said.

"You haven't told us what happened to Archer and his beloved Jenna." B said,

"That very probably is not for you to know, since it falls on the next pages. It's true I implied they went back to the states to The Pilgrim's Way old-soldiers-for-Christ home near San Francisco and I can assure you they spent splendid afternoons emailing grandchildren and dreaming about Jesus's sure embrace if catastrophe should ensue. And we know from inside, that catastrophe always ensues, but if we're lucky, only catastrophe and not atrocity. No more atrocity to dog poor Archer's flame-blasted brain. So the frequent charge that I write about people no one finds either caring or companionable or in any way sympathetic may not be justified."

"I like your use of 'may not' there." A said.

"I like my use of B's lesions here," C said. "You'll have to be careful not to get your wretched blister fluid on your phone. That would surely sabotage your deepest desires."

"You don't have the faintest idea of my desires."

"I control them all. Bring them to the page, or not, as I wish."

B said, "You find some deranged affirmation in imagining you imagine the world. But self-obsessed music captivates no one. And you end up facing your actual undertaking: returning utterly alone to the states to do what? Ruminate about how much better things were over here? Or maybe to sink into a slow depression of too many longed-for returns. Maybe my lesions would be blessed relief."

"I wouldn't argue with me; your lesions might only be the beginning. I can make you howl like a partially run-over dog, stuck to the pavement by his own blood and squashed intestinal tubing. So yowl, please, upon my command."

"I do not yowl upon command."

"Maybe these lunches have served their purpose and we should bid each other adieu," A said.

"I'll let you know. Indeed, you'll be the first to know when the next page is empty. Or at least you're not there."

"We will be there, or rather, here, no matter what you decide. We inhabit this place as much as you do."

"Not if you don't show up on the next page."

"You keep saying that, like some crummy litany, but we'll be here next month sipping our green tea, wiping our hands on microwaved mini towels and debating starters. We might even remember you."

"If I allot you memories. And I must say I'm not inclined to. How would they advance anything?"

"How do you advance anything? Why shouldn't I take a shovel edge to you right now?"

And as the conversation burrowed more deeply along this narrow track of emotional disdain and fear, Serena's door opened and Madame Vincouvier and Monsignor Fulton came in together. They were an astonishing pair, she in ebony near toile, and he in maroon cape over orange flashing vestments.

"We're here because neither of us find a stupid argument over the making of fiction versus the living of life an honest way to conclude this tiresome book," the Monsignor said resonantly.

"Yes, "Madame Vincouvier echoed, "it's childish to decide who has greater reality: the one writing; or the one written about. Neither has credibility. It's boring diversion. And the cardinal rule of all diversion is to avoid boredom. Look at you—grown men arguing who gets to be on the next page, as if any of you had that kind of authority—"

C said, "I can claim that kind of authority. I snuffed out Daisy before anyone knew anything about you."

"Daisy was my cat," A insisted. "I held her as she died."

"Only because I wrote about it," C said. "Only as I allowed you care, just as now I bequeath lesions to him." C pointed to B.

"I don't see any lesions on my arms or legs, you little turd of a writer."

"Just turn the page."

And together they did so.

159

www.ingramcontent.com/pod-product-compliance
Lightning Source LLC
Chambersburg PA
CBHW050408030726
47503CB00006B/2075

About The Author

Joab Stieglitz was born and raised in Warren, New Jersey. He is an Application Consultant for a software company and also a notary signing agent. He lives in Alexandria, Virginia.

Joab is an avid tabletop RPG player and game master of horror, espionage, fantasy, and science fiction genres.

Joab channeled his role-playing experiences in the Utgarda Series, of pulp adventure novels with Lovecraftian influences set in the 1920's.

You can follow Joab on Twitter @JoabStieglitz, and on his blog: joabstieglitzbooks.com.

JOAB STIEGLITZ

THE OLD MAN'S
REQUEST

BOOK ONE OF THE UTGARDA SERIES

The Old Man's Request
Book One of the Utgarda Series

Fifty years ago, a group of college friends dabbled in the occult and released a malign presence on the world. Now, on his deathbed, the last of the students, now a trustee of Reister University enlists the aid of three newcomers to banish the thing they summoned.

Russian anthropologist Anna Rykov, doctor Harry Lamb, and Father Sean O'Malley are all indebted the ailing trustee for their positions. Together, they pursue the knowledge and resources needed to perform the ritual.

Hampered by the old man's greedy son, the wizened director of the university library, and a private investigator with a troubled past, can they perform the ritual and banish the entity?

The Old Man's Request is a pulp adventure set in the 1920s, and the first book in the Utgarda Series.

Available in paperback and ebook formats, and as an Audible audiobook

THE
MISSING
MEDIUM

BOOK TWO OF THE UTGARDA SERIES

JOAB STIEGLITZ

The Missing Medium
Book Two of the Utgarda Series

While Father Sean O'Malley is summoned to Rome to discuss the "Longborough Affair" with his superiors, Russian anthropologist Anna Rykov and Doctor Harold Lamb travel to New York City where they encounter merchants, mobsters and madmen in pursuit of the spirit medium who advised their mentor shortly before the start of the whole adventure.

The Missing Medium is a pulp adventure set in the 1920s, and the second book in the Utgarda Series.

Available in paperback and ebook formats, and as an Audible audiobook

THE OTHER REALM

BOOK THREE OF THE UTGARDA SERIES

JOAB STIEGLITZ

The Other Realm
Book Three of the Utgarda Series

Having discovered the location of Brian Teplow, Russian anthropologist Anna Rykov, doctor Harry Lamb, and Father Sean O'Malley travel to a secluded asylum to collect him. But things are not so simple, and Anna must travel to the land of Teplow's imagination to rescue him, where she finds a different world from the one suggested in the Missing Medium's journals.

The Other Realm is a pulp adventure set in the 1920s, and the third book in the Utgarda Series.

Available in paperback and ebook formats, and as an Audible audiobook

THE HUNTER
IN THE
SHAD●WS

BOOK ONE OF THE THULE TRILOGY

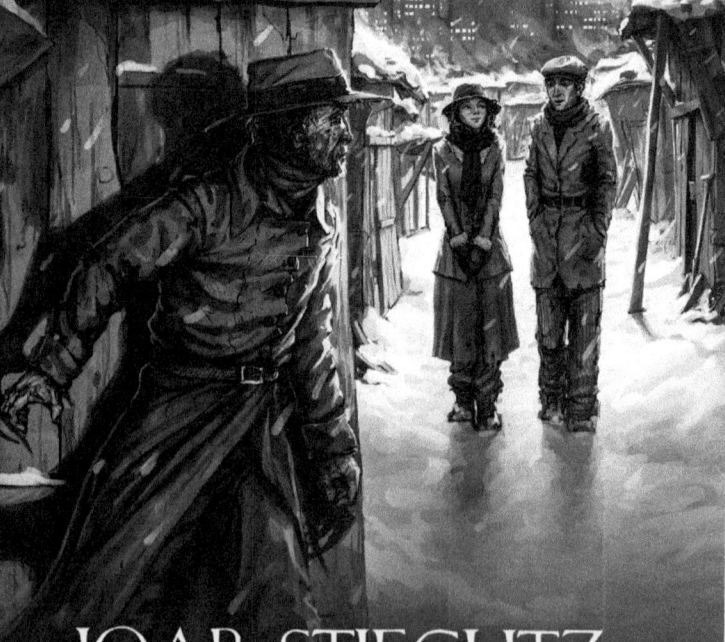

JOAB STIEGLITZ

The Hunter in the Shadows
Book One of the Thule Trilogy

After dreaming that her alter-dimensional sister Sobak was in danger, Anna Rykov is sent to Depression era Boston to find and kill the shape shifting alien who has captured her, and whose plans could bring about the extinction of all life on Earth

Anna is assisted by Cletus the hound and a homeless World War I veteran with skeletons in his own closet. However, Anna's inquiries catch the attention of J. Edgar Hoover, whose motives in this case are unknown.

The Hunter in the Shadows is a pulp adventure set in the 1930s, is the first book in the Thule Trilogy, and the fourth book in the Utgarda Series.

Available in paperback and ebook formats, and as an Audible audiobook

THE
WORLDS
I KNOW

Book Two of the Thule Trilogy

JOAB STIEGLITZ

The Worlds I Know
Book Two of the Thule Trilogy

With the discovery of a plot by the German Thule Society to seed alien chaos in the western powers, Anna is summoned to England to investigate mysterious runes uncovered during a mining survey.

But her arrival in England is not well received by British authorities, and the subsequent inspection of the site takes Anna to a familiar place, Siashutara, the world seen by psychic Brian Teplow and documented in his childhood journals. This Siashutara, however, has been updated to modern times, and Anna is the heretic scion of Nygof, the assassin whose actions caused the global upheaval known as the Cataclysm. She finds herself as the prisoner of the fanatical theocracy that succeeded Queen Sif of Brynn, Anna's ancient foe, and all her colleagues from Earth now have alter-egos there as well.

The fate of both Earth and Siashutara are at stake. Anna must escape and figure out how to stop the two worlds from merging into one and restore them to their own paths.

Reversing The Cataclysm

Book Three of the Thule Trilogy

Joab Stieglitz

Reversing the Cataclysm
Book Three of the Thule Trilogy

When Anna Rykov pursued Brian Teplow, the spiritualist that her benefactor has spoken to before his death, to the world of Siashutara, she inadvertently entered the conflict between two warring alien species competing to see their preferred version of the timeline come to fruition.

Having seen both ancient and modern Siashutara, Anna has come to learn that her interference in the past caused the upheaval in Siashutara known as the Cataclysm and initiated the merging of Anna's reality and this Other Realm.

Now Anna must convince her colleagues, alter-egos of people she knows in the "real world," to help her to undo her meddling and restore both worlds to their original paths. To do so, Anna will need to travel into the Jungles of Niahaut and convince the God-King of the Haut to send her back to the past, where she must travel on the journey as originally described in the medium's boyhood journals.

But even if he agrees to her request and she follows all the rules as originally described, will it be enough to alter the timeline and reverse the Cataclysm? Or will her intrusion only cause more problems with the fabric of time?

www.ingramcontent.com/pod-product-compliance
Lightning Source LLC
Chambersburg PA
CBHW050404030726
47503CB00006B/2013